BULLETPROOF

THE UNBREAKABLE SERIES

BOOK 3

MELISSA SEAL

editors@emerald-books.com

BISAC Categories:
FIC027210   FICTION / Romance / LGBT / Lesbian
FIC031010   FICTION / Thrillers / Crime

Series: Unbreakable Book 3

Summary:
Melissa Seal's third and final book in the Unbreakable series sets the stage for an emotional reunion for the characters we have come to know and love. Readers will get an up close and personal view of a betrayal so damaging and its impact on Dani, Lexie, and everyone around them. It's an emotional rollercoaster you won't want to miss.

emerald-books.com

EMERALD
BOOKS

PRAISE FOR UNBREAKABLE

BOOK ONE OF THE UNBREAKABLE SERIES

★ ★ ★ ★ ★ **Crimes, shock, and love triangle**

Great first book from a debut author! The book has the twists and turns of a crime thriller with a touch of a love story that has you wondering what will win out. Will it be love or the judgement of society and the obstacles life puts in the way?

DEDICATION

This book is dedicated to Rebecca Stohler, without whom this book would never have been written. Her guidance and constant support have helped shape me into the writer I am today.

Preface

Dani tossed and turned all night thinking about the gorgeous blond. *Lexie, baby, I don't know what to do. I like Callie, but I'm still head over heels in love with you. I don't think that's ever going to change.*

Early the next morning, she went down to the river with Alex hoping for some clarity. The sun was barely up, and she noticed Jolene talking to two men in black suits.

What's going on there, I wonder. Is she in trouble?

Dani continued to observe the heated conversation between the woman and the two government goons until Jolene walked away, wiping tears from her green eyes. She pulled her hat down and looked away as she walked past Alex and Dani. Dani took the baby and went to breakfast. After breakfast, mom and daughter went back to the cabin to get Ellie. They planned to spend the day in Yellowstone National Park, which was about a thirty-minute drive.

Driving away from the ranch, she saw Jolene get into a black SUV with government plates along with the two men. *I hope everything is alright with Jolene.*

Alex sang along with Disney songs, and Dani thought about her new friend with the flowing blond hair and intense blue eyes. They entered the park and followed the crowd to the welcome center. She was overwhelmed with all the information about the park.

Dani put Alex in the stroller. "Okay, kiddo. Your mama really wanted to visit this place, so let's take it all in and tell her all about it when we say our prayers tonight."

"Okay, Mommy. I will tell Mama all about the park." Lexie had a list of the things she wanted to see when they visited Yellowstone, so they used her list as a guide. Dani chose the Cascade Lake trail in the Canyon Village area first. The path was roughly five miles and an estimated two- to three-hour hike. They stopped at the waterfall and took pictures. The landscape was breathtaking, and it made Dani's heart yearn for her late wife.

This is hard to do without you babe, but I know you are watching over us and that makes it a little easier.

The list included watching Old Faithful, the geyser that erupted every ninety minutes. They wanted to get a look at the Grand Prismatic Spring. The colors captivated Dani. The center was the same blue as Lexie's eyes, and the fiery oranges and reds reminded her of Lexie's passion for justice. They took a scenic boat ride on Yellowstone Lake and then retired to their room at the Lake Yellowstone Hotel. There was too much ground to cover in one day. Dani fell asleep thinking of Callie and wondering how she was doing.

Alex and Ellie woke at the crack of dawn excited to continue their tour of the National Park. The next day's agenda included Gibbon Falls, which turned out to be impressive. Next up was the Mammoth Hot Springs Terrace, with over fifty hot springs in that area. They ventured on another hike where they saw two grizzly bears, some bison, a fox, and several wolves. Dani was a little uneasy with all the wildlife running around. Still, she stayed the course, and the tour ended with an old-fashioned, Western cookout. The guests traveled on a covered wagon through sagebrush flats the same way they did in the Wild West. Once they arrived at the barbecue, they enjoyed an excellent meal before heading back to the ranch.

It was late when Dani pulled up to the cabin. Alex had slept since they left Yellowstone. The past week at the ranch had been too much for Dani. Everything reminded her of Lexie and visiting all the places without her only made her feel worse. She tried her best to keep it together for Alex, but it was harder by the minute.

She put Alex to bed and asked, "El, would you mind hanging out here for a bit? I need to take a walk." Her friend agreed to stay with Alex so Dani wandered out into the chilly night. She sat on the ground, gazing up at the stars.

"It's so hard to believe you left us one year ago. I've had my year of firsts, and I have to say, it sucked. I took Alex trick-or-treating dressed as a police officer for the first time without you. We spent our first Thanksgiving without you. We set a place at the table for you, which only made me miss you more. I got through my first Christmas and Valentine's Day without you. Your birthday and Mother's Day were excruciating, and now here I am in one of your favorite places without you on the first anniversary of your death. Why you and not me? You could've handled this life better, and you would have been a better parent. I should have listened to you when you asked me to quit the fire department and travel the world with you. Maybe you would still be here and we would be enjoying this place together. Everything is all messed up, Lex, for the past year I've sleepwalked through my life until this week. I met a girl that makes me feel alive again."

"I'm here, babe. Dani, I'm right here," spoke a voice in the darkness. The sweet sound sent chills throughout her body, and she stood to face the darkness. Her breath caught as she watched her heart walk out of the shadows. She nearly fainted when she got a close look at her late wife.

Am I dreaming? If so, please don't wake me up.

Dani stood frozen in place, astonished as Lexie walked slowly to her. Her hair was red and her eyes were green, but there was no mistaking her voice. Jolene was Lexie. Before Dani could process what was happening, she heard Callie calling her name.

Callie rushed towards her. "Hi there, I stopped by the cabin. Ellie told me you out here." Callie didn't know the other woman was there as she continued to talk to Dani. "I've been thinking about you non-stop for the past two days. I know this may not be the perfect time, but these past few weeks have been the best of my life. You have an unexplainable effect on me. Dani, I think I'm falling in love with you."

CHAPTER 1

Lexie awoke in a dimly lit hospital room surrounded by a doctor, two men in FBI jackets, and a woman wearing a U.S. Marshal jacket. She saw them huddled in a corner of the room, whispering. She spoke weakly to let the group know she was awake.

The doctor was the first to reply, "Welcome back, Detective. You gave us quite a scare. My name is Dr. Rebecca Barnes, and these agents are here to keep you safe."

Lexie tried to sit up, but the pain was overwhelming.

"Keep me safe from what? I don't understand. Where is my daughter? Is she hurt? Where is my wife?" inquired a confused Lexie.

Dr. Barnes laid a gentle hand on her patient's shoulder.

"Don't move around too much right now. You sustained quite a few internal injuries and some major burns. We stopped all the internal bleeding and wrapped your wounds. You will make a full recovery, but you have to take it easy for a bit." Explained the doctor.

One of the men spoke up, "My name is Randy Kessler. I'm a special agent with the FBI. Your family is currently at your funeral. Everyone but the four people in this room believe you died in that car accident."

Lexie rubbed her temples, "This makes no sense. Why would my family be at my funeral? Clearly, I am not dead."

"Coach Patterson hired someone to kill you, Lexie, and if he thinks you are dead, Alex and Dani will be safe. If Patterson finds out you are alive, he will come after you again, and he will not stop until you are dead. Do you understand, Lexie?" clarified Agent Emily Harper of the U.S Marshals. "Once the doctor says you are well enough to travel, we will relocate you to a safe place. There cannot be any contact with anyone from your past until Patterson is locked away or dead."

"This is bullshit and completely insane! Where is my phone? I'm calling Dani now! How do you expect me to let my family believe I'm dead? I have a daughter, for crying out loud. Am I supposed to ride off into the sunset while they grieve?" snapped Lexie.

Agent Harper sympathized with Lexie. She sat next to her bed and placed her hand over the detective's and spoke softly to her.

"I'm sorry, Lexie, but that can't happen unless you want to place a target on your family. I know this is scary and exceedingly difficult, but you must stay strong and brave for your girls."

Harper handed Lexie an envelope, "Here is your new identity and destination. You haven't been cleared by the doctors to fly yet. They think it will take a few more days here for you to be medically sound for relocation. I will stay with you until you are well enough to go."

Lexie was not compliant at all. She angrily tried to fight her way out of the room, but she was too weak to even get out of bed. The doctor sedated her for her own safety.

One week later, Lexie was loaded onto a government plane, and when she woke, she was at the Wyoming ranch. After many conversations with the agents, she finally agreed that she needed to stay hidden away for everyone's safety.

Lexie was miserable at the ranch, and she hated looking in the mirror and seeing the red hair and green eyes that were forced on her by the Marshal's office. She missed her wife and daughter so much that sometimes she thought it would be better if she had died in that car crash. She worked at the ranch and tried to settle into her new life; however, she was lonely and despondent.

A few weeks into her new life, Lexie went to the local bar and drank way too much. She ran into a somewhat familiar face from the ranch who was on a mission to drink her cares away, too. They were drunk and lonely. They ended up half-naked together in a bathroom stall. It wasn't until the woman spoke that Lexie realized what she was doing. Lexie immediately stopped and ran out of the bathroom, leaving the perplexed woman alone.

Lexie didn't want some random stranger touching her. She wanted Dani, and she was going to do whatever it took to get back to her. Lexie immediately decided that she would do her job and try to enjoy being at the ranch for the sake of her sanity. She went to work the following day with a brand new attitude. Lexie found the woman she had been with the night before and apologized for her behavior. The woman insisted Lexie had no reason to apologize, and they could simply remain coworkers.

Within a few months, Lexie ran the daily activities for the guests. She was going on trail rides with experienced riders and teaching the inexperienced riders the ropes. She was white water rafting and hiking mountains. If Dani and Alex had been there, Lexie could have fallen in love with life at the ranch.

Lexie spent the next few months settling in and learning how to become Jolene, the sassy redheaded activities director who loved adventure. She threw herself into her work in an attempt to draw her focus from her life with Dani and Alex. Lexie fought the urge to contact them every single day. She pushed her body to the breaking point every time she went out so that she could sleep at night. The agony of losing her family was worse at night when it was quiet, and all the memories flooded in.

Chapter 2

"Good morning, everyone. It's a great day for a hike," beamed Lexie. "My name is Jolene, and I will be your guide for this incredible adventure. It is essential that everyone stay together during this hike. There are many dangerous areas you will need to be aware of, not to mention the wildlife. Please stay with the group, and listen to the guides."

Lexie settled into her role as Jolene. The guests loved her and waited in line for hours for one of her hiking tours.

"This is my favorite part of the day. I love listening to the faint sound of birds chirping as the golden rays of sunshine fill the sky. Such a peaceful feeling."

The temperature for the day was sixty degrees and sunny, which was perfect weather for hiking through the Teton Mountain range.

"Today, we are going take an extremely tough hike up to the Static Peak Divide. We will go close to twelve miles. Remember, stay on the trail and with the group."

Most of the hikers on this trip were experienced, but there were a couple of newbies. The hike was scheduled to take seven to eight hours depending on how much time the hikers wanted to spend at the rest points to enjoy the view and take pictures. This trail had quickly become one of Lexie's favorites. She especially loved the insanely high hills that made her calves feel like they were on fire until she reached the top. The view was magnificent. She couldn't describe what she felt when she stood on top of the mountain. This was the only place Lexie felt true happiness.

The group reached the top of the mountain, and their guide was planning a rest break for them when she heard a loud scream. One of the newbies had ventured a little too close to the side of the trail. The hiker attempted to take a selfie when the ground shifted, and she slid off the side of the mountain. Lexie moved quickly to the area where the fallen woman hung on to a branch.

"Don't move. I'm coming down to get you," instructed Lexie.

Lexie was in total control of the situation, and everyone was in awe of how calm their guide was. She attached a rope around a tree and began her descent. The hiker had fallen a good twenty feet before latching onto a branch, and Lexie was by her side in minutes.

"Are you hurt?"

The woman whimpered, "My leg hurts pretty badly."

"I'm going to make a harness with this rope and place it around you. All you have to do is hold on to me, and we will get you up safely and get that leg checked out," explained Lexie.

Lexie placed the harness around the woman, but the woman flinched when Lexie touched the injured leg, causing the harness to fall a hundred feet into the thick brush below.

Dammit! Now what? Lexie tried to figure out how to get the woman up safely without a harness.

"Okay, listen to me carefully. I'm going to untie my rope and tie it around your waist, and Tommy is going to pull you up."

Lexie yelled up to Tommy, one of the other guides. "The harness fell, so I'm putting my rope on Jessie here, and you are going to pull her up. Once you have her up safely, then you will toss the rope back down to me and pull me back up."

"I don't think that's the best idea, Jolene. What if you can't hold on long enough for me to get the rope back down to you?" inquired a concerned Tommy.

"Just do it, Tommy. I'll be fine. She is ready. Start pulling her up."

Bracing himself against a tree for better leverage, Tommy thought, *Damn girl, you are unapologetically fearless. I waited my whole life to meet a woman like you.*

Lexie had no sooner gotten the words out when the branch she stood on broke, and she tumbled into the thick brush. She felt herself falling, and then she felt nothing until she woke up in the rescue chopper.

Tommy was by her side in the chopper.

"What happened?" asked Lexie.

"The branch you were standing on snapped, causing you to fall about twenty feet. The paramedics said you have a concussion, and you suffered some serious bruising. Still, it doesn't look like you broke anything. We won't know for sure until you get checked out at the hospital."

CHAPTER 3

The week following the hike, Lexie was told to stay in bed and rest as much as possible. She was groggy from the pain medicine. The doctor at the hospital told her she didn't have any broken bones or internal bleeding. Just some massive bruising to most of her lower body. Even with the medicine, her entire body ached from the fall.

She was almost asleep when there was a knock at her door. "Who is it?" she asked weakly.

"Hey Jolene, it's Tommy. I thought you might be hungry, so I stopped by the café and picked up some soup for you."

I am hungry, and some soup would be good. Lexie rolled herself out of bed and opened the door for the young ranch hand.

"Thanks, Tommy. I appreciate you bringing this over."

Tommy smiled shyly, "Would you like some company?"

"Not tonight. I don't feel up to it. I'll see you tomorrow." Lexie replied as she gently closed the door.

Tommy walked away with his head hung down. *What do I have to do to get this woman to take me seriously? Those mesmerizing green eyes haunt my sleep.*

After devouring the homemade chicken noodle soup Tommy brought her, Lexie cozied up with her pillow and blanket on the couch to watch a movie. Halfway through the film, she was drifting off to sleep when her cell phone rang. *What now? Agent Harper's office is the only one who has this number? Maybe she is calling to tell me Patterson has been arrested!*

"Good evening Jolene. This is Agent Harper."

"I know who this is, Harper. No one else has this number."

"Well, then I will get straight to the point. Dani, Ellie, and Alex are on their way to the ranch. They should be there in the next couple of days. You need to remain out of sight and away from them. Do you understand?"

"What? Why are they coming here?" demanded a confused Lexie.

"Apparently, they are on some long road trip, and Wyoming is their next stop. Are you going to be able to handle this?"

"Absolutely not. The minute I see her, I'm going to fall apart and most likely run to her."

"You know that's not an option, Lexie, and you need to understand that this is serious. Take some time off and go away for a week or so. They should not arrive for a few days. You have time to get away."

"You know this is utter bullshit, don't you? You force me to let my family think I am dead. Then you move me thousands of miles away to the middle of nowhere. You turn me into a redheaded, green-eyed ranch hand, and now you want me to take a vacation. What the fuck, Harper?"

Lexie tossed and turned for hours, and when she finally fell asleep, she dreamt of Dani all night. When the alarm rang the following day, Lexie was determined to go to work. *There is no way I can stay in this cabin alone with my thoughts another day. I will call Dani for sure if I don't get something to take my mind off her.* She managed to drag herself to her office, where she found Tommy and Callie getting things ready for the day.

"Good morning, you two. Thanks for standing in for me while I was out."

Callie looked confused, "I thought you fell off a mountain a week ago. Should you be back at work already?"

"I can't do anything strenuous for a while, but I can still do the administrative stuff."

Tommy headed to the stables to get ready for the day's first trail ride while Callie met her group for white water rafting. It was October, and the river was freezing, but the guests could still enjoy an action-packed ride with the wetsuits.

Lexie was going over the trail riding schedule for the week when she saw the car pull up. She froze when she saw the familiar woman jump out of the passenger's seat and run toward the entrance. *Ellie? Shit! They aren't supposed to arrive for another couple of days.* She saw Dani in the driver's seat and got dizzy like she couldn't breathe. Her mind couldn't comprehend what her eyes saw. *Dani? Alex? Oh my God, my entire world is within arm's reach, and I can't let them see me!* She pulled her brown cowboy hat down and quickly walked out of the building and away from the woman she had loved and lost. Lexie passed Ellie as she looked down at the ground, practically running away from the newly arriving guests.

Bumping into Tommy on her way out of the building, Jolene mentioned, "Tommy, I've got an errand to run. Can you get the new guests checked in and take them to their cabin? I will be back in about an hour."

"I got you covered, Boss. I will take great care of the new guests."

Lexie bolted out the door, stopping only when she reached her cabin. She fiddled with the keys to the cabin. She couldn't get the key in the lock because her hands were shaking so badly. Inside the cabin, the distraught woman sat at the kitchen table, staring at a picture of her, Alex, and Dani as tears streamed down her face.

Lexie managed to pull herself together just as her phone rang, making her cringe.

"I am sorry, but it looks like they will be there today. I thought you would have time to leave the ranch before they showed up. We need you to understand you cannot have any contact with them." reminded Agent Harper.

"I know the fucking rules, Agent. You don't have to keep explaining it to me. My family believes I'm dead, and that's the way it will stay."

CHAPTER 4

Lexie spent the rest of the night alone fighting tears and the urge to reveal herself to Dani. *How can anyone expect me to stay away from them? That's my whole world within my reach. Why can't I tell them I am here? I'm doing it. Fuck Agent Harper and her stupid ass rules!* Lexie was hyped up and ready to go find Dani when there was a knock at her door. She looked out the window and saw a black SUV parked in her driveway. *Well, wonderful!* She opened the door and ushered in Agent Harper.

"I suspect you may have a little trouble following protocol this time. I came to offer my assistance." smiled Harper.

"I don't want or need your assistance, Agent," hissed Lexie.

"Let's take a drive and get your mind off of everything," offered Agent Harper.

Lexie internally cringed. *Why yes, Agent Dipshit, let's go for a drive. Because that will absolutely make me forget that my wife and child are here, and I can't talk to them or touch them.*

Agent Harper and Lexie drove to a nearby bar. They listened to the jukebox while Lexie poured out her heart to the only person that had been a constant in her life since her "death." Harper listened as Lexie stumbled through a range of emotions about her current situation.

Harper encouraged the brokenhearted woman to hang in there, "The Norfolk Police Department and FBI are working diligently to put Coach Patterson and his gang away for good. I need you to hear me and understand the severity of your situation. Three weeks ago, Patterson and his henchmen murdered a six-year-old on the playground simply to send a message to the child's father."

"What was the message, and why is that bastard still free?"

"We believe the boy was killed because his father was slated to testify against Patterson in a few months. Patterson is an extremely dangerous and intelligent man. Even though we know he did it, there is no evidence, and he has a rock-solid alibi. People are so afraid of him; they will do whatever he asks. He will, without a doubt, kill your entire family, starting with Alex, if he finds out you are alive. Right now, he believes you died in that car accident, and no one is looking to pin your murder on him. Dani and Alex are safe. He has no reason to mess with them. So, please do not put a target on your family."

Once Agent Harper was satisfied Lexie was in a better headspace, she drove her back to the ranch.

"Call me if you need to talk. I understand this is hard for you, but just remember the big picture is putting Patterson behind bars and getting you back to your family." encouraged Harper.

Lexie watched from a distance as Dani, Alex, and Ellie settled in at the ranch. They seemed so happy without her. She watched Alex squeal with delight when she saw the ducks in the lake and heard Dani laugh when Ellie fell in the water trying to reach the ducks. It was one of her most painful experiences, but she understood she needed to stay away for their safety.

The following week was challenging as Lexie fought her every impulse and watched her family enjoying their life as if she never existed. She was angry all the time and wanted to murder Callie, who was spending way too much time with Dani. Even though it was Callie's job as Lexie's assistant to make sure the guests were happy and well taken care of.

Two weeks after Dani arrived at the ranch, Lexie received a call from Agent Harper.

"I'm so sick of this woman calling," huffed Lexie as she answered. "What now? I haven't gone anywhere near Dani or Alex."

"Good morning, Jolene. We have some things we need to discuss with you. A driver will pick you up and bring you to a secure location where we can talk about your future. He should be pulling up to your cabin now. I will see you shortly."

The young agent attempted to talk to Lexie, but she was in no mood. The annoyed woman opened the door and let the U.S. Marshal escort her to the black SUV. They rode in silence for an hour until they reached their destination.

Walking into the building, Lexie wondered, *what now? Are they going to tell me I have to relocate again? I hate this, and I just want it to be over.*

The young agent escorted her from the SUV into the building. He guided her into a small office with a desk and two chairs. "Please take a seat here. Agent Harper will be here any minute."

Lexie sat in the chair facing the desk and waited. After a few minutes, the bubbly U.S. Marshal came sauntering into the room. Lexie hated to admit it, but she kind of liked the woman. She reminded her of her best friend Debbie, whom she still missed terribly.

"Hello there," smiled Harper. "I have some excellent news for you today. It seems Coach Patterson and his top-tier people were all killed last night in a raid by the FBI and Norfolk PD."

"Great question, glad you asked." Harper paused for a second and then continued, "What does this mean for you? It means you are free to go back to your life. You can go right now to your wife, who is still at the ranch, and tell her everything you have been waiting to say."

Lexie was in shock. "Is this real? The threat to my family is gone, and I can go back home?"

"Yes, Lexie, this is as real as it gets. Thank you for your sacrifice. I wish you the best with your family and in all your future endeavors. Agent Scott will drive you back to the ranch."

The Marshal handed her a package, "This is for you unless you would like to stay in Wyoming as Jolene."

Lexie took the envelope and hugged the woman who had been the most constant person in her life over the past year. "I'm going to miss you, Harper, but not enough to stay. Thanks for everything. See you around."

Agent Scott was waiting in the vehicle when Lexie came out grinning.

"I think that is the first time I have ever seen you smile," noted Scott.

"This is the first time I've had a reason to smile."

Lexie sat back and thought about what she would say to Dani. She would be back at the ranch in an hour and planned to go straight to Dani's cabin. Lexie opened the envelope Harper had given her to find a new driver's license with the name Alexandra Williams.

CHAPTER 5

While rushing to find Dani, Lexie ran into Callie coming out of her wife's cabin. Both women were confused to see the other.

"What are you doing here?" questioned Callie.

Lexie responded, "Not that it is any of your business, but I need to speak with Dani. Is she here?"

"No, she isn't here. She took Ellie and Alex to Yellowstone yesterday. They will be back later tonight. I was just leaving some fresh linens for them."

The two women went their separate ways, each thinking of the one woman they were both in love with. Callie walked back to the front office to work until Tommy came to relieve her at eleven. She planned to go see Dani and tell her she was falling in love with her. *I know it's crazy to feel this way after only two weeks, but I can't help how I feel. It will probably make Dani run for the hills when I tell her. However, I would hate myself if I let her leave this ranch without knowing how I feel.*

Lexie called the ranger station and asked them to call her when Dani left Yellowstone. She knew how long the drive back to the ranch took, and she wanted to be ready when Dani got back. She showered and took out the green contacts. For the first time in over a year, she looked in the mirror and almost recognized herself.

It was almost 9:30 pm when Lexie received the call that Dani was on her way back to the ranch. It would be 10:30 pm before they returned, and she was so excited she couldn't stand still. Lexie had dreamed about this moment every night since the day she left, and now it was finally here. She was nervous, scared, and excited.

Callie saw Dani's car drive past the front office just as Tommy came in to relieve her. She grabbed her jacket and ran straight to Dani's cabin. Ellie informed her that Dani was taking a walk by the river.

Lexie showed up and heard Dani talking to *her*. It broke Lexie's heart to hear the pain in Dani's voice. "We finally made it to the ranch, and now I see why you wanted to come here. This place is amazing. We have only been here for a week, but I feel like I could stay here forever. I only wish we could be here together, Lex. I miss you so much."

"We *are* here together, Dani," announced Lexie from the shadows of the woods. Before Dani had time to process what she heard, Callie showed up.

Callie told Dani that she was falling for her, and she wanted a chance to get to know her better. Dani couldn't focus on anything Callie said. Finally, after what seemed like forever, Lexie walked out of the wood line.

"Lexie!" gasped Dani.

"Jolene, what the hell are you doing here, and why is she calling you Lexie?" demanded a confused Callie.

All three women mutely absorbed what had just happened. Dani realized Lexie was alive and that Callie was in love with her. Lexie realized Callie was in love with her wife, and she may have lost Dani. Callie realizing Jolene was Dani's "dead" wife.

Dani tilted her head quizzically at the sound of the familiar voice. Lexie approached her, and Dani froze in place with an expression of bewilderment. Unsure what to do or say, Callie gracefully dismissed herself and ran back to her cottage. *What are the freaking odds that her dead wife is hiding out at a ranch in Wyoming and is my boss? This is too bizarre.*

Lexie pulled Dani into an enormous hug as the tears flowed from her unusually vulnerable blue eyes.

Dani melted into Lexie's loving embrace until Lexie spoke, "Are you okay, my love?"

Pulling away, Dani's eyes blazed as she fought back the tears, "Am I okay? No, Lexie, I am *not* okay. What the hell are *you* doing in Wyoming? Why is your hair red, and why does everyone here know you as Jolene? Most importantly, why did you let me believe you died?!"

Unable to handle her intense range of emotions, Dani attempted to leave, but Lexie wouldn't let her. After several minutes of begging, Dani agreed to stay and hear Lexie out. There was a chill in the night air, but neither woman noticed it as they spent the next few hours standing by the river. Lexie tried desperately to make Dani understand why she had to fake her death. Every word Lexie said only made her wife angrier.

"Lexie, this is bullshit. You shouldn't have made a decision that affects our family without talking to me about it. You could have trusted me, Lex. Do you have any idea how hard it was to keep going after your funeral? I damn near died with you. Did you even stop to think about what this was going to do to Alex and me?"

"I'm sorry, babe, but they didn't allow me to contact you until now!" cried Lexie. "Every day, I had to fight the urge to call you. It was the absolute hardest thing I have ever done, but I knew it was safer if everyone believed I was dead."

Dani wiped the tears from Lexie's face and pulled her close. She inhaled the familiar scent of the woman she had thought she was going to spend the rest of her life with.

"Have you been alone the entire time?" asked Dani. She didn't really want to hear Lexie's answer, but she felt she needed to know.

Lexie hesitated before answering, "We don't need to talk about that now. Tell me about Alex."

"I spent the last year of my life mourning the loss of my wife. Getting up each day was a battle I nearly lost. I never once thought about another woman, only you. So yes, we do need to talk about this right now. Were you with someone else over the past year, and do not lie to me again, Lexie."

"Yes, I was with someone else briefly, but let me explain," pleaded Lexie.

Dani felt like she had been gut-punched, "I don't want to hear any more explanations from you. I didn't so much as look at another person, and I thought you were dead. You had an affair knowing I was mourning you. That's great, Lex. At least now I know what I truly mean to you."

Lexie tried to hug her wife, but Dani pulled away. "I'm beyond happy you are here and safe, Lex, but I'm not ready to forgive you for the hell you put us through. I may never be ready."

"I understand, Dani, but promise me you won't go see Callie tonight. You are hurt and confused, and she will take advantage of that. We are still married."

Frustrated, Dani took a deep breath, "Are you freaking kidding me, woman? You gave up on our marriage when

29

you let me believe you were dead. Did you remember your wedding vows when you were sleeping with this other person? You have no right to ask me not to see her or anyone else."

Chapter 6

Walking back to her cabin, Dani called Callie to let her know she needed some time to process everything and asked if they could talk tomorrow. Callie was disappointed but wanted to be supportive, so she wished Dani a good night and promised to stop by the next day.

Dani barely made it to the cabin's front door before she fell to her knees in tears. Ellie ran to her friend, and Dani looked up at her with trembling lips and, in a shaky voice, explained, "Lexie is alive. She has been living here at the ranch."

Ellie couldn't help herself. Her jaw dropped to the floor as her eyes shot open wide, "What are you talking about? That makes no sense at all."

Dani pulled herself up from the floor with clenched jaws, and she repeated, "My wife is not dead. Her coffin is empty. She has been in witness protection since the car accident. Lexie is Jolene, the activities director here. I just talked to her down by the river. Apparently, the threat is over, and she was given permission to return to her life."

Ellie's mouth opened, but she couldn't find the words. Instead, she hugged her best friend and held her while she cried herself to sleep. The trauma of losing Lexie and then finding out she was still alive was too much for Dani. She was emotionally drained, and Ellie hated Lexie for doing this to her friend. *As soon as Dani goes to sleep, I am going to find that lying heifer.*

Lexie heard banging on her door and assumed it was Callie. She was fully prepared to beat that bitch down if necessary. She was not giving Dani up without a fight. Opening the door, Lexie was greeted with a slap across the face.

"This is a whole new level of insanity. What is wrong with you? Why would you even tell Dani you are alive? She was just coming out of the darkness *you* created when you left! Damn you, Lexie, for hurting her yet again. If you ever loved her or Alex, you would walk away again and this time for good."

Before Lexie could defend herself, Ellie turned and stormed off. Lexie followed, chasing the woman down. She caught up with Ellie before she got out of the driveway.

"Ellie, please just listen to me for a minute. This wasn't my doing. I had no control of the situation. Dani has to understand, I would never leave her or Alex unless I was forced to do so."

Lexie pleaded, but Ellie didn't want to hear anything she had to say. As far as she was concerned, Lexie had abandoned her family, and she didn't deserve a second chance.

The following day Dani woke with a headache, a crying child, and a missing best friend. Ellie came into the cabin as Dani tried to soothe Alex.

"Good morning, Ellie. Where did you go so early?"

"I went for a walk with Tommy. He wanted to watch the sunrise. I would've left a note, but I thought I would be back before you guys woke up. What's going on with Alex this morning?"

"I'm not sure. She was crying earlier but seems fine now. Do you mind staying with Alex while I shower and go see Callie?" asked Dani.

Ellie picked Alex up and swung her around, "It would be my pleasure to hang out with this little munchkin. What are you going to do about Lexie?"

Dani's eyes blazed with anger, "I'm not ready to deal with her yet, but she will want to see Alex soon, though, so I guess I better get ready."

CHAPTER 7

Dani walked the mile from her cabin to Callie's to clear her mind. Callie was on the back deck drinking coffee and watching the birds when she saw Dani walking up. Callie sprinted eagerly across the yard and jumped in Dani's arms.

"Well, hello there," grinned Dani.

"Hi gorgeous," replied Callie.

"Can we go inside?" inquired Dani.

Callie placed her hand in the small of Dani's back and gently guided her into the cabin. Once inside, Callie made them both a cup of coffee.

"Go ahead and say it, Dani." encouraged Callie as she tried to hide the hurt in her voice. She knew what the woman had come to say, and she just wanted the conversation over.

"I wish I could say I was here with better news, but unfortunately, I have an undead wife to deal with, and it's complicated because we have Alex. I have enjoyed getting to know you over these past few weeks, but I can't get romantically involved with anyone right now."

Dani kissed Callie on the forehead before leaving. "I'm truly sorry, Callie. I'm in uncharted waters here. I have only known you for a few weeks, and she is my wife. I don't know if I can ever forgive Lexie or let her back in my life, but I do know that until I figure this all out, I can't start anything with you."

"I honestly can't say that I understand what you are going through, but I do understand your need for space to work your stuff out. I am disappointed, but I wish you and your wife the best of luck in working this mess out."

Dani looked at her phone for the first time that day and noticed she had seven missed calls from an unknown number and three from Ellie. She called Ellie to see if Alex was okay.

Ellie answered the phone on the first ring, "That must have been some conversation if it lasted for three hours.

Lexie has been to the cabin demanding to see Alex. I didn't know what to do, so I told her she would have to talk to you. She was angry, but she left and asked that you call her."

"I'll call her now. Sorry, you had to deal with her. I will take it from here."

Dani dialed the number Ellie gave her, and Lexie answered immediately.

"Where's your cabin?" inquired Dani. "I will come to you. There are some things we need to discuss before I let you see Alex."

"My cabin is the one across the road from Callie's. I'll be waiting for you."

Lexie was waiting on the front porch when Dani pulled up. Lexie noticed Callie watching them from her window, but she chose to ignore her for now. Dani parked her car and walked toward her wife. Her hands were sweating, and her heart was pounding. Lexie stood to hug Dani, and the younger woman allowed it.

They stood holding one another for a while before Lexie mentioned, "I have missed you so much, babe. It feels amazing to have you in my arms again."

"I have missed you too, Lex. I don't know if I can ever trust you again. I need you to understand that the sting of your betrayal is not something I can simply get over. I'm thrilled that you are alive, but I came here to talk about Alex, that's it."

The women went inside the sparsely decorated cabin. Dani noticed a small picture of the three of them taken at the park right after the wedding. The silence was deafening as they each tried to find the words to express how they felt.

Lexie finally broke the silence. "How's Alex doing?"

"Considering she lost her mom when she was only two and half years old, she is doing well. She misses you, and sometimes she wakes up crying and can't tell me why. I know it's because you aren't there."

The women settled into a familiar routine as they discussed their child. Dani filled Lexie in on everything she has missed concerning Alex. Things were going great until Lexie asked Dani personal questions.

"I told you I was only here to talk about Alex. She is our daughter, and she misses you. She deserves to know you, and I'm willing to make that happen, but I'm not willing to talk about us or rekindle anything with you. You had to preserve your lie, and it cost you our relationship. I will in no way keep you from our daughter, but I don't trust you with my heart anymore."

Lexie's heart sank as Dani told her she did not want to be with her. "Are you serious right now, babe? I love you more than you will ever be able to wrap your head around. I did all of this to protect you and Alex."

Dani was dismissive and determined not to argue with Lexie.

"I understand this is more than a one sitting conversation Lex, but I need time to sort out my feelings. You can't just pop up after being "dead" for a year and assume we can pick up where we left off." sobbed Dani.

Dani didn't want Lexie to see her cry, but the smorgasbord of emotion she had battled since last night finally won. Dani crumbled to the floor as Lexie bent to comfort her.

Dani blubbered, "I stared at your picture so much that I memorized the details of your face, and I saw it every time I closed my eyes. There wasn't one moment over the past year where I felt whole. The pain was crippling. There were days when I literally could not get out of bed because missing you was excruciating."

"I am so sorry, sweetie. I did it to keep you and Alex safe," whimpered Lexie as she held the sobbing woman.

After a few minutes, Dani pulled herself together. "You can come see Alex later tonight, but I need space. I will be there for Alex, and that's all."

Chapter 8

L exie showed up at the cabin, excited to see her daughter. She was worried Alex wouldn't remember her, but Dani assured her that was not the case. Dani had shown Alex pictures of the three of them every night before bed and told her stories about Lexie. Dani was confident Alex would know who she was the minute she saw Lexie.

Alex heard the knock on the door, "Mommy, someone is at the door."

"Thank you, Bug. I will go see who it is."

Alex squealed and jumped in her Momma's waiting arms. "Momma, you are here. I missed you, Momma! Where have you been?" The toddler buried her head in Lexie's chest and held on to her mom for dear life.

Dani couldn't help but smile. Even though she was angry and hurt, she wanted Alex to be happy, and she was genuinely delighted Lexie was back. Alex wouldn't let Lexie out of her sight the rest of the evening. The three of them played together and made dinner. They were finishing dinner when Dani's cell phone rang. She stepped outside to take the call. Lexie was reading a story to Alex when Dani returned.

"Was that Callie?" questioned Lexie.

"Yes. She wanted to come over to talk, but I told her you were here spending time with Alex."

"Thank you for doing that," smiled Lexie.

"I didn't do it for you, Lex. I did it for Alex."

Lexie spent the evening loving every second of getting reacquainted with her daughter. She tucked Alex in and told her a few bedtime stories. Once the toddler was asleep, she hoped to get some alone time with Dani, but that didn't happen. Lexie came out of the child's room and found Dani talking to Callie in the living room. The ladies had made the decision to be friends.

"Alex is sleeping, so I guess I should go now."

"I think that's a good idea. You want to come over to-morrow and go hiking with us?" invited Dani.

"I would love to. See you in the morning. Thank you."

Lexie was torn between the excitement of seeing Alex and the devastation of losing Dani. She couldn't bear going back to her depressing cabin all alone, so instead, she walked to the river. It was easily her favorite place on the ranch. The cool breeze touched her softly as a faint smile made its way across her face. *Dani may hate me, but my baby girl still loves her momma.*

While at the river, Lexie realized she was so focused on Dani that she almost forgot about all the other people she left behind. She made a mental list of all the people she needed to contact. Her parents, Debbie, and Captain Harris were the people Lexie wanted to call first. Everyone else she could talk to when she got back to Virginia. Lexie took out her cell phone and called her best friend, Debbie.

After three highly emotional conversations, Lexie's best friend, parents, and Captain knew that she was alive. She told them all the same thing she had told Dani. Only they were all happy she was alive, and no one was mad at her. Debbie told her not to worry. Dani would come around; she just needed some time to process it all.

Captain Harris was over the moon that his best detective was returning. He couldn't wait to have her back on the streets solving cases and keeping the rest of the Violent Crimes Division on track. Debbie booked a flight to Wyoming so Lexie wouldn't be alone.

After talking to everyone and realizing she was loved and missed, Lexie felt better and could return to her cabin. She fell asleep that night holding a stuffed animal Alex had given her. She woke before the alarm and waited outside the cabin when Alex and Dani came out ready for the hike.

On the way back from the hike, Lexie asked, "Would you let Alex come with me to the airport tomorrow? Debbie is flying in, and there is a park near the airport that I think Alex will like."

"How long has Debbie known you were alive?"

"I called her last night after I left you guys," answered Lexie. "She bought a plane ticket while we were on the phone. She is actually excited to see me. So, what about Alex?"

"You can have Alex for the day tomorrow. Just try and have her back by bedtime."

Lexie took Alex to the park while they waited for Debbie's plane to arrive. The mother-daughter duo enjoyed feeding the ducks and swinging on the swings. They played and laughed like the past year never happened. Alex loved the woman who had saved her, and she was delighted to have her back.

Debbie exited the plane terminal and nearly passed out when she saw Lexie holding Alex. Although she knew Lexie was alive, the reality didn't set in until she saw her friend in person.

"My goodness, Lexie, I love the fiery red hair. It is so good to see you!" exclaimed Debbie.

"It's great to see you, my friend. I have truly missed you."

The ladies and Alex spent the day together, reconnecting. By the end of the night, Lexie was ready to say goodbye to the ranch. The next morning, she gathered everyone that worked at the ranch and told them the truth about who she was and that she would be leaving.

Everyone was sad to see her go but happy she could get back to her real life. They wanted to throw her a going-away party, but Lexie just wanted to get on the road. She was desperate to get to Virginia and get her life back. They were planning to leave the day after tomorrow. Tomorrow, Lexie wanted to take Debbie and Alex on a tour of all her favorite places at the ranch. Dani was planning to spend the day with Callie while Tommy and Ellie spent the day together.

Alex was wide awake at six the next morning, waiting for her momma to come to pick her up. Lexie was there right on time, and they spent the day wandering all over the ranch. They went on trail rides, short hikes, and Alex fed the barn animals. At the end of the night, Lexie took Alex back to Dani's cabin and was disappointed when Dani didn't ask her to come in.

Debbie was busy packing Lexie's things back at her cabin so they could head out first thing the following day. Lexie was in tears when she entered the cabin.

"Was she there?" inquired Debbie.

"Yep. My wife is falling in love with her life without me, and I don't know what to do. I'm not ready to give up on our marriage. I love Dani."

"Dani feels betrayed right now. She will come to her senses as soon as she gets back home," encouraged Debbie while handing her friend a glass of wine. "Let's get this stuff packed up and get some sleep."

CHAPTER 9

Although Lexie wanted to spend every second with her daughter, she agreed to let Alex ride back with Dani. Lexie's one condition was that Dani agreed to joint custody while they worked things out. Lexie was confident that she and Dani would be back together very soon, so she was willing to give Dani all the space she needed.

The drive from the ranch to her parent's house in Norfolk took two days. The women drove continuously, stopping only for food and gas. Lexie wanted to get home as fast as she could. She needed to see all the people who loved and grieved her, so she could apologize for the hurt she caused them.

Lexie pulled the pickup into the driveway of the modern two-story house her parents bought when they moved to Virginia. It was ten in the morning, and both women were exhausted and in need of a bath.

Paul Williams was the first to see the truck pull up. "Mary! She is here! Our baby girl is home!"

Mary Williams was cleaning the breakfast dishes when she heard her husband's excited screams. Her parents were at the truck before she put it in the park. They practically ripped their daughter out of her vehicle. *This is how I expected my wife to act when she saw me. Has she truly fallen out of love with me?*

Lexie spent the next few days catching up on everything she had missed. She was staying with her parents for now. The house was large enough for her and Alex to have their own space, and Lexie had missed her parents terribly over the past year. She was planning to stay there until Dani was ready for her move back in with her and Alex.

Soon after returning home, Lexie wanted to go back to work. She had a meeting scheduled with Captain Harris. Hopefully, Lexie would be back at work in another week or two if she passed her psych evaluation. They needed to know that the year she was in witness protection had not taken a toll on her mentally and that she was mentally and emotionally ready to return to active duty.

The meeting with Captain Harris did not go as well as Lexie hoped. She was under the impression that all she needed to do was see the police psychologist and answer a few questions to be reinstated. Lexie was devastated to learn that she had to attend a minimum of twelve office visits with the shrink before an accurate evaluation was possible.

"Twelve sessions, Cap, really? That will take at least three months," whined Lexie.

"I understand you are frustrated, but policy is policy. You can take this time to get reacquainted with your family and friends. There is no need to rush, Detective. The criminals are not going anywhere."

"How soon can I get started?"

"I'm glad you asked. Your first appointment is scheduled for tomorrow morning at 9am."

Not knowing what to expect, Lexie showed up twenty minutes early for her appointment. Realizing she was early, the detective decided to get a cup of coffee from the coffee cart outside the building. Her phone buzzed as she walked out the door, causing her to bump into a woman holding coffee in one hand and bagels in the other.

The woman's coffee spilled all over her, and the bagels fell to the ground.

"Oh, my goodness, I am so sorry. Let me buy you another cup and replace the bagels." offered a contrite Lexie.

"No worries. I was planning to cut back on my caffeine intake this week anyway. So, essentially, you did me a favor."

"No, seriously, let me replace it, please."

"I would love to, but I'm running late and have to get upstairs. Don't worry about me or the spilled coffee. Have a good rest of your day." dismissed the stranger before she disappeared into the building.

Before getting in line for the coffee cart, Lexie glanced at her watch and realized she only had a few minutes to get to her appointment. The elevator took too long, so she chose to take the stairs to the third floor. Arriving at the office door, Lexie took a deep breath, composed herself, and walked in to find an empty desk.

Thinking she was in the wrong place, Lexie turned to walk out and ran smack into the same woman from the coffee cart. This time, the stranger was carrying an arm full of papers and a cup of orange juice that spilled all over the documents.

"Damn it. I knew I should have called in sick today," fussed the woman.

Lexie was mortified she had bumped into this woman again and caused her to spill her second beverage that morning. She stood frozen, waiting for the woman to stop ranting. When she looked up, the woman noticed Lexie from downstairs and introduced herself.

"I'm Dr. Stevens. Are you my nine o'clock appointment?"

"Yes, ma'am. I'm Lexie Williams, and again, I am so sorry."

"Please don't apologize anymore, Detective. I should apologize to you for not being here when you arrived. I had a run-in with this clumsy chic at the coffee cart," smiled Dr. Stevens. "Come on in and have a seat. Give me a second to get this mess cleaned up, and we can begin."

Lexie helped the doctor clean up the papers and spilled orange juice before sitting on the comfortable, plush blue couch and waiting for the doctor to begin.

CHAPTER 10

"Today is the day everything changes. Today they will see you for what you really are. You see, Mattie boy, this is the end for you, but just the beginning for me. It's time to take back my life and end yours."

Forty-eight hours ago, Matthew Stanton was night fishing at the lake near his childhood home when he was violently abducted. The former sailor spent a lot of time fishing since his discharge from the Navy three months ago. Matthew hated being back home in New Jersey, living with his parents. His father yelled at him and told him he was worthless all the time. His mother was drunk constantly, and his girlfriend was upset about Matthew losing the steady paycheck he had shared with her.

Standing on the riverbank, the young man thought about jumping in and just letting the river take all his pain away. Before he could jump, he was hit in the head and woke up bound, gagged, and naked on a cold concrete floor. *Well, this is perfect. I will never have to go back to the fucking house ever again.*

His captor strolled in wearing a black hoodie and black ski mask. Matthew didn't squirm or try to get away at all. He looked into the eyes of his torturer and accepted his fate.

"Kill me. I don't deserve to live!" cried Matthew.

"No, you do not deserve to live, and I promise you won't survive this, but you will suffer immensely before this night is over."

The killer took out all the necessary tools to complete the upcoming execution.

"Okay, Mattie, let's get this party started, shall we?"

Over the next two hours, Matthew Stanton's body was stabbed, beaten, soaked in acid, and he was set free with one final stab.

The killer stood over his limp body and spit on it, "Someone should have taught you to make better choices, Mattie. To be a better man. Rot in hell, bastard."

Chapter 11

Lexie got through her first two months of visits with Dr. Stevens with minimal effort. She showed up, answered questions, and told the doctor what she wanted to hear. Lexie had kept the psychologist at bay for the time being, and she looked forward to today's session. Only four more sessions and she would be back to work.

Lexie bounced into the office, beaming. "Good morning, Doc. How's it going?"

"Good morning. Let's jump right in. Today, I want to talk about your marriage and how it has been affected by your choices."

Lexie paused briefly before speaking,

"My choices? Nothing that has happened since the car accident has been my choice. Faking my death, changing my name, moving to Wyoming, none of it was my choice."

Dr. Stevens was excellent at her job, and she knew this was a touchy subject for the detective, but she also knew it needed to be addressed.

"So, you feel like this all happened to you. You had no control at all? It was not your choice to keep Dani in the dark about your death?"

Lexie did not like the direction this conversation was going. She excused herself to use the restroom. *Okay, Lexie, you just have to get through this the best you can. It will be over soon, and you can go back to work. Focus on the endgame.*

Returning from the restroom, Lexie gathered all her strength before speaking. "In answer to your last question, yes, I do feel like this all happened to me, and I was absolutely powerless. The FBI and U.S. Marshal dictated my every move. It was not my choice to keep Dani in the dark. It was out of my control."

Knowing it was necessary for her patient's healing, Dr. Stevens continued to push Lexie. "How is your relationship with your wife now that you are back? What is your living arrangement? Has she welcomed you back with open arms?"

With a smile on her face, Lexie answered, "Our relationship is tumultuous at the moment, but we are working things out. I am staying with my parents for now until Dani is ready for me to come home. She will come around. Dani just needs time. She still loves me and wants us to be a family. I am not worried at all. Dani understands everything I did was to protect her and Alex."

"Let's talk about Alex. What was her reaction to you being alive? Did she understand what was happening when she saw you for the first time ?"

Lexie talked to Dr. Stevens for the next thirty minutes about her reunion with her daughter. Lexie was happy to talk about her daughter. Her eyes lit up when she remembered seeing Alex for the first time at the ranch. She explained how wonderful it felt to hold Alex again. She explained that seeing her baby girl again was the most incredible feeling in the world and knowing that she was safe made all her sacrifices worth it.

"Okay, Lexie, it's time for you to get real with yourself. You have contradicted yourself several times when answering my questions. You claim you have no responsibility for what the FBI and U.S. Marshal made you do, and Dani understands that. You also state that even though your relationship with your wife is tumultuous, you truly believe she will take you back. If I bring Dani in to talk with us, will she say the same?" pushed Dr. Stevens.

Choking back sobs, Lexie finally admitted, "Dani doesn't understand, and she is not willing to even talk to me. We talk about Alex. That's it. She feels betrayed and hurt. I pray every day for her to forgive me and let me back in, but I'm not sure she ever will."

All at once, Lexie lowered the walls she had built over the past year and let the tears flow. She told the doctor all her fears about losing Dani and how isolated she felt in Witness Protection. Dr. Stevens allowed the woman the time she needed to get it all out. She offered a shoulder to cry on and some tissues. Other than that, she let Lexie do all the work.

With the floodgates now open, Lexie was on the road to healing, which was precisely what she needed to be reinstated. It was a tough hour, but it made Lexie face the reality that Dani may not want her back. It was a harsh reality, but one that Lexie understood was a possibility.

Lexie thanked Dr. Stevens for the session and promised to see her the following week.

Walking to her car, Lexie thought, *what bullshit. I will play your game Doc, but I know Dani will forgive me, and we will be a family again.*

CHAPTER 12

Three months after leaving the witness protection program, Lexie passed her psych evaluation with flying colors and was reinstated to active duty as a Norfolk detective with the Violent Crimes Division. Detective Jordan Carr was beyond thrilled to have his partner back.

He scooped her up into a giant bear hug the second she stepped into the office. "Well, look who's back from the dead! It's super to have you back, partner. This past year has been horrible without you."

"I'm happy to see you, too, Jordan. I missed your stupid face." teased Lexie.

Her first day back was insane. She barely made it in the building before she and Carr were called out to a crime scene. The detectives pulled up in their unmarked sedan two blocks from their destination. The streets were filled with patrol cars with flashing lights and crowds of concerned citizens. Walking the two blocks to the crime scene, they found the body of a young white male draped over a blood-stained mermaid statue. Red crime scene tape blocked access to the statue as they waited for the medical examiner to remove the victim.

"Can someone please cover the body?" requested Lexie.

The patrol officer who was first on the scene came over to brief the detectives. "A woman on her way to work at City Hall noticed the body and called 911. First, on the scene, we arrived a few minutes after the call. The caller was nowhere to be found. We secured the scene, and then you guys arrived," reported Officer Reynolds. "It's really great to see you, Detective Williams."

"It's great to be seen, Reynolds, and I missed you, too," grinned Lexie.

Haley Thomas, the newest medical examiner, was there to process the body. Haley had joined the Norfolk Police Department a few months after Lexie's death. She knew all about the feisty detective from her fellow officers, and she was excited to see what the fuss was about.

Jordan introduced Haley and Lexie, and then Lexie asked, "Can you tell us how he died?"

"It's an honor to meet you, Detective. I've heard so much about you, and I'm looking forward to working with you. As for your victim, all I can say with any certainty is that your victim is missing an important part of his anatomy."

Lexie took control of the investigation with all the confidence of the seasoned detective that she was before she became a ranch hand. They canvassed the area searching for the woman who called 911. After hours of searching and attempting to put the pieces together, the detectives went to see the medical examiner.

Captain Harris met them there and informed them, "The victim is twenty-five-year-old Matthew Stanton. Stanton is originally from New Jersey. He came to Virginia by way of the Navy and was recently discharged. You two should coordinate with the Navy to see if you can find out more about the victim."

"So, do you know the cause of death?" inquired Lexie.

"Your victim bled out from being stabbed over fifty times and having his penis cut off. The death stab was the one in his right shoulder. Three major arteries are running through that shoulder. Once his attacker hit that, he would have bled out quickly. That was the last stab wound."

Jordan thanked Haley, and the detectives went back to the police station to continue their investigation. Matthew's parents and girlfriend were on the way from New Jersey to identify the body.

"It will be around four this afternoon before the victim's family arrives. We should see if we can speak to his commander at the naval base before they get here," explained Lexie.

They drove to Oceana to speak with Senior Chief Petty Officer Rowe, Stanton's Senior Chief. The man was distant and cold.

He refused to answer any questions and told the detectives, "That piece of shit is no longer the Navy's problem. I have nothing else to say about this matter. Please see yourselves out."

Lexie was frustrated, "It seems like the Senior Chief was not a huge fan of our victim."

"I wonder what that's all about. According to his personnel records, he was never in trouble or anything. It just looks like he joined, did his four years, and got out. A lot of people do that," Jordan mused.

By the end of her shift, Lexie was exhausted. She had forgotten the physical and emotional toll this job took. Nevertheless, Lexie was ecstatic to be back. She was having dinner in an hour with Alex and Dani. The women were not back together, but they were doing their best to make things as normal as possible for Alex.

Alex spent half her time with Dani and the other half with Lexie, but they tried to spend time together as a family when they could. It had only been a month since Lexie's resurrection. Dani was still not ready to talk to her about anything that didn't involve their daughter. So, Lexie was caught off guard when Dani asked her to stay after they put Alex to bed that night.

Dani was quiet until Lexie sat down beside her on the sofa. She was so close Dani could smell the coconut shampoo Lexie used. *If I don't say this right now, I may never be able to say it.* "Callie is coming to visit me in two weeks. She will be staying in an Airbnb for about a month."

"What the fuck, Dani? Why is she moving from Wyoming to Virginia? You *do* realize that we are still married, don't you? What's going on with you two anyway? Do you love her?"

"Whoa, crazy lady, calm down. First of all, she isn't moving here. She is visiting and has her own place to stay. Secondly, no, I do not love her, but I do like her. We have been talking on the phone almost every day and have gotten close. She wants a change, and she doesn't have any family left in Wyoming. Her only living relatives are in Richmond. Last but not least, don't forget you left me, and I had to learn to live without you. Maybe a new friend is just what I need."

"I think you are making a huge mistake, Danielle. I love you, and I will not stop fighting for us. So, you can hang out with your new bestie all you want, but you are just putting off the inevitable. You and I will be back together in our house with our daughter." Lexie leaned in and kissed Dani gently on the top of her head before leaving.

CHAPTER 13

The next few weeks flew by for Lexie. She and Jordan were working diligently to find Matthew Stanton's killer. Lexie did all she could to remain calm the day Dani picked Callie up from the airport. It was a Friday, and Lexie would pick up their daughter in the morning. Alex would be spending the weekend with Lexie while Dani was on a forty-eight-hour shift at the firehouse.

It was a cold, rainy day, and Lexie planned a movie day for her and Alex. They were going to watch all of Alex's favorite Disney movies. Mom and daughter had looked forward to it all week. Halfway through their third movie, Lexie's phone rang.

"Hey, Jordan. What's going on?"

"Sorry to bother you. I know this is your weekend with your daughter, but we have another Mermaid Murder."

"Seriously, Jordan. Mermaid Murder. Where did you get that from?"

Jordan laughed, "The media has dubbed this guy the Mermaid Murderer. I'll meet you at the station. I know you need to get Alex to your mom's."

Lexie called her mom and then packed Alex up. The toddler was disappointed but happy to see her grandmother. Lexie hated leaving Alex, but she needed to catch this newest psychopath. *There are over twenty-five of these freaking mermaids all over this city. Is this guy planning to drape a body over all of them?*

Arriving at the crime scene, they saw another male body draped over a mermaid statue.

Lexie inquired, "What do we have here?"

Officer Cornett replied, "Unknown black male with a missing penis. The body was found completely nude with no identification. His prints were sent in, so we should have an ID soon. The medical examiner is on the way."

"Thanks, Officer. Can you point us to the person who found the body?" asked Jordan.

"A female called 911, but there was no one here when we arrived," replied Cornett.

Lexie and Jordan made sure the scene was secured, then they went to pull video footage from the surveillance cameras.

"Do you think it's weird that both of these Mermaid Murders were called in by an unknown female who can't be found?" inquired Jordan.

"I think it's very coincidental for sure. Maybe we should listen to the 911 calls to see if it's the same voice," suggested Lexie.

Jordan turned the vehicle around and headed for the dispatch office. Entering the dispatch office, Lexie asked to listen to the 911 call from 7:15 that morning.

"911 operator. What's the nature of your emergency?"

"There is a man hanging off of the mermaid statue on 11th street."

"Can you tell if the man is injured?"

"I think he is dead. There is blood everywhere."

"I have dispatched a unit to your location with paramedics. Can you tell me your name?"

Noticing the confused looks on the faces of the two Detectives, the lead dispatcher spoke up, "After we asked for her name, the caller immediately disconnected just like the first call."

The detectives listened to both the 911 calls and noted the similarities in the caller's voice. The caller had used a disposable phone, so it couldn't be tracked.

"I think our killer may be a woman," stated Lexie.

"You think the same woman making the 911 calls is the one killing these men? She would have to be pretty strong to get the bodies placed on those mermaids."

Back at the station, the second victim had been identified as thirty-year-old Robert Baker from Maryland. Mr. Baker was recently discharged from the Navy as well.

"Okay, now this can't be a coincidence. Two dead victims both recently discharged from the Navy, and both stripped naked for the world to see," noted Jordan.

Lexie replied, "It seems like the killer is trying to make a statement by cutting off their man parts and putting them on display."

The detectives went back to the station to gather all the information they could on their victims. Matthew Stanton and Robert Baker had both been stationed at Naval Station Norfolk for the past four years. They were both deployed on the same ship. The ship returned to Norfolk six months ago. Both sailors received a general discharge three months after returning from sea.

"I think there is something the Navy doesn't want us to know. I'm going back to try to find someone who will talk to me," announced Lexie.

"I'll drive," said Jordan.

They ran into roadblock after roadblock until they were just about to give up and leave. A young female petty officer met them in the parking lot and handed Jordan a piece of paper with a telephone number. The note read, *Call this number at midnight tonight. I have information.*

Lexie's eyes lit up after reading the note. "This could be the break we were looking for. I've got to pick Alex up. We can meet back at the station around eleven-thirty and make the call."

"Sounds good. Tell Alex hi for me," replied Jordan.

Mary Williams was playing Candy Land with her granddaughter when Lexie showed up.

Once they finished their game, Lexie inquired, "Mom, is it okay for Alex to spend the night here? Jordan and I are working the Mermaid Murder case, and we have a new lead. I have enough time to have dinner with you guys and give Alex her bath and put her to bed."

"Of course, my dear. Alex can stay as long as you need her to. Please be safe out there."

CHAPTER 14

J ordan made the call at precisely five minutes after midnight, but there was no answer. The call went straight to voicemail. He tried to call three more times, and each time the call went straight to voicemail. Realizing no one was going to answer that phone, Lexie called the phone company to get a name for the mysterious young girl.

"The woman's name is Madison Price. She is a seaman at Naval Station Norfolk. We need to get over there and make sure she is okay," announced Lexie.

"Oh, the senior chief is going to love seeing us again. Especially at one in the morning," quipped Jordan.

This time, they went to the barracks hoping to find Madison. They saw a group of sailors in the hallway looking frantic. "Hey guys, what's going on?" asked Jordan.

"Madi is missing!" screamed one girl.

Lexie calmly asked, "Why do you think she is missing?"

She spoke up with tears flowing, "She was supposed to meet me at midnight after her shift, and she never showed up. Madi is never late without letting me know, and she would never just *not* show up. She wanted to tell me something tonight. I went to her barracks room, and it's a mess, which is not like Madi at all."

"Take me to the barracks room," ordered Jordan.

The detectives entered the barracks room to find books and papers strewn all over the floor, and some pictures looked as if they had been knocked off the wall. There were definite signs of a struggle.

"When was the last time anyone saw or talked to Madison?" questioned Lexie.

Before anyone could answer, Senior Chief Rowe showed up. "Everyone in their barracks room. Now."

The sailors didn't hesitate at all. They scrambled to get in their rooms.

"How can I help you today, detectives?" asked Rowe.

"We are looking for Madison Price. According to the group of sailors you just banished, Madison is missing. Do you know where she might be?" asked Lexie.

"Seaman Price is on a mission. She was sent out on a ship earlier tonight. That is all I can tell you people about the mission. I will have Price contact you when she returns. And Detectives, please do not speak to my sailors again without my permission."

Annoyed by the constant roadblocks from the senior chief, Lexie responded, "We need a list of names of all the sailors that were in this hallway tonight. We will be bringing them in for questioning. Also, we will need to contact Madison Price on the ship to confirm her whereabouts."

Rowe was furious, "I don't think you understand how this works, missy. You and your little buddy here need to leave my base and *do not* come back. We have our own police here, and if there is anything that needs investigating, they will do it. You can leave now, or I can have the Master-at-Arms come and escort you off base. The choice is yours."

The detectives realized there was nothing more they could do until morning, so they called it a night. Lexie went to her parent's house, took a shower, and crawled in bed with her daughter. *This world is a scary place, and it terrifies me to let you out in it.* Lexie wrapped her arms around her sleeping child and fell asleep.

Chapter 15

Dani picked Callie up from the airport, and for the first time since Lexie's "death," she felt at peace. The two women chatted easily on the way to the Airbnb. Callie filled Dani in on all the happenings at the ranch while Dani talked about Alex and the firehouse.

Arriving at the Airbnb, Callie noticed the swimming pool, "You should bring Alex over for a swim later."

"I can bring her over tomorrow afternoon. She is with Lexie today."

"Well, then maybe you and I could go for a swim later tonight," suggested Callie seductively.

Dani grinned, "Maybe."

The two women had gotten closer over the past three months. They talked for hours on the phone. They would watch movies together on Facetime or just talk about everything and nothing simultaneously. Dani felt comfortable with Callie and enjoyed their conversations.

After walking around the backyard and checking out the pool, they went inside to find a beautifully decorated living room. Anxious to see how Dani would react, Callie suggested they check out the bedroom.

"I'm sorry, Callie, but I have to get to the firehouse soon, so I'd better head out now. I will call you later. It's good to see you."

Disappointed, Callie walked Dani to the door. "It's good to see you, too. I can't wait to see Alex. Have a safe day at work."

Callie spent the rest of the day shopping for food and toys for Alex. The girl had turned four years old two months ago, and Callie wanted to give her a birthday gift in person. She and Alex would talk on video chat when Alex was with Dani. She was a bright, sweet kid, and Callie enjoyed chatting with her.

Dani showed up at the firehouse three hours before her shift and ran into Piper.

"What are you doing here so early? Our shift doesn't start for a few more hours." inquired Piper.

"Callie came to visit today, and I know what she wants, and I'm afraid," whispered Dani.

"Afraid of what?" asked Piper.

"Of letting Lexie go. Of getting involved with Callie. Getting my heart broken again."

Doing the only thing she knew to do, Piper told Dani to change into her running gear, and the firefighters went for a three-mile run before their shift. Dani was always active, but running became the only way she could cope with her grief after Lexie died. Some days she woke up unable to breathe before running four or five miles.

Piper and Dani ran through the park and down by the water. They were lost in their own thoughts for the duration of the run.

Once they were back at the firehouse, Dani finally spoke, "Thanks, Lieutenant. I feel much better now. I'm going to hit the showers before our shift starts."

After showering and getting dressed for work, Dani called Callie to check in.

Callie answered right away, "Hi there. How was your meeting?"

Dani felt guilty about lying about having a meeting, but she was committed to the lie now. "It was boring but necessary. How are you settling in?"

"The house is fantastic, and I love the pool. I went to the grocery store earlier. I'm going to fix lasagna and a salad."

"Yummy. Sounds delicious. I wouldn't mind if you wanted to come to the firehouse and have dinner with me."

Callie smiled, "I will see you in a few hours."

The firefighters at Station Sixty-one enjoyed a good evening filled with training and lots of laughter until the alarm sounded. Dani realized it was almost time for Callie to show up with homemade lasagna. *Dang, it. I was really looking forward to that homemade lasagna dinner with Callie tonight.*

Callie pulled in just as the fire trucks rolled out. She locked eyes with Dani, and the firefighter mouthed, "Sorry. I'll call later."

The firefighters rushed to the site of a vehicle fire in an abandoned shopping center parking lot. Arriving at the scene, Dani, Max, and Piper exited the fire trucks. They put the fire out swiftly and were loaded back on the truck, unaware of the stranger watching them.

They arrived back at the station just before midnight, and Dani wanted to call Callie but thought she might be sleeping. Having missed dinner due to the vehicle fire, everyone was starving.

"Whose night is it to cook?" inquired Max.

"What's that heavenly smell?" asked Piper.

Walking into the kitchen, the hungry firefighters found a woman making them dinner.

Callie smiled when she saw Dani. "I thought you all might be hungry. I have some lasagna and salad. Who wants some?"

After Dani introduced Callie to everyone, they all sat down to a delicious home-cooked meal. *I could definitely get used to having you around,* thought Dani as she watched Callie chat easily with the other firefighters.

CHAPTER 16

Several days after Callie's visit to the fire station, Dani and Alex spent the day with Callie. It was a hot, muggy summer day, and all three of them looked forward to spending the day in the pool. Dani arrived right on time. Her punctuality was one of the things Callie loved about her. She was a woman of her word and always showed up.

Alex wanted to go swimming as soon as they arrived. Dani managed to contain the child's excitement long enough to put sunscreen on her. After Alex was smothered in sunscreen, Callie jumped in the pool with Alex right behind her. The young girl had learned to swim at an early age and loved being in the water.

The trio swam and played Marco Polo until Alex was worn out. After enjoying her grilled cheese and fresh fruit, Dani put Alex down for a nap and rejoined Callie in the pool.

"Did Alex fight you on the nap?" asked Callie.

"Nope. She was so tired. I actually think she wanted to take a nap."

Callie was lying on a cactus-shaped float when Dani swam under her and knocked the unsuspecting woman into the water. Callie came up laughing, and they tousled over the float until it slipped away from them. With the pool float gone, Dani found herself so close to Callie that she felt her breath on her cheek. She was suddenly aware of her desire for the other woman.

Callie knew the time was right as she leaned in and softly kissed Dani. "Is this okay?"

"This is okay," smiled Dani as she pulled Callie into another more passionate kiss.

Alex woke up from her nap and called for her mommy.

Reluctantly Dani pulled away from Callie. "We should get out now. I promised Alex we would take her to get ice cream if she ate all her lunch. I'm sure she will want to go now that her nap is over."

Callie smirked, "Ice cream sounds great. I need to cool myself off anyway."

Dani sent Alex to find her shoes, then turned to Callie, "I need for us to take this slow. Alex needs to see us as just friends for now. Can you handle that?"

"I'm in no hurry, Dani. We can take it as slow as you need, and as far as Alex is concerned, I will honor your wishes. Now, let's go get some ice cream."

Dani was paying for their ice cream when she heard Alex squeal. She turned to see Alex hugging her granddaddy.

"Well, hello there, sweet granddaughter," said Mr. Williams. "Who is your friend?"

"This is Callie. She is Mommy's friend and mine too. We went swimming in her pool today. Now we are getting ice cream."

"Hi, Callie. I'm Lexie's dad. It's nice to meet you. I should get in the line before it gets much longer. Grandma gets cranky without her afternoon strawberry shake."

Dani stopped and briefly chatted with her father-in-law before returning to her table, where Alex was telling Callie knock-knock jokes. *It's great that they get along so well.*

After leaving the ice cream shop, the trio took Callie on a walking tour of the city. They visited as much of the town as they could before stopping at a small pizzeria for dinner. They were all exhausted by the time they dropped Callie off at her Airbnb. Since Alex was sleeping soundly in the backseat, Dani stepped out of the car to say goodnight to her new girlfriend.

"So, are we actually going to try to do this?" asked Callie.

"If you can handle taking it slow, and if you are okay with Lexie being in my life because she always will be. She is Alex's mother, and I want to have a good relationship with her for Alex's sake."

Callie sighed, "I understand all of that, but I do have one question concerning Lexie. How long do you plan to stay married to her? I'm not asking nor expecting you to file for divorce today. However, I would like to know where your head is on this subject."

"Not too much longer. I have already spoken to an attorney about how to get the process started."

Hearing Alex stir, she kissed Callie and told her she would call her in the morning.

CHAPTER 17

It was Lexie's weekend with Alex, and summer was in full swing. The city was up in arms over the Mermaid Murders and the police department's lack of a suspect. Lexie was overwhelmed at work and frustrated with only seeing Alex on designated days. She hated not being able to see her every day. Lexie was trying to be patient with Dani and let her find her way back in her own time.

One morning, Lexie was busy packing the car for an impromptu weekend at Myrtle Beach with Alex. She was picking her up from Dani's house in an hour. Lexie needed to get away and spend time with her daughter. The hotel was booked, and she couldn't wait to get Alex and get the hell out of Norfolk.

As she grabbed the last of the luggage from her closet, Lexie heard a knock at the door. *Who is here this early on a Saturday morning? It better not be Jordan.*

Lexie opened the door to find a young man in a suit and tie holding a manila envelope. "Good morning, ma'am. Are you Alexandra Williams?"

"Yes. I am. Who are you?" asked a confused Lexie.

The young man handed her the envelope, "You've been served," said the man who hurried to leave.

Served? What the hell am I being served?

Lexie opened the envelope and quickly realized she had just been served with divorce papers. She physically felt her heartbreak at the thought of losing Dani forever, but she knew she needed to let her go. It had been six months since she came back to Norfolk, and in that time, Dani hadn't given her any indication that she wanted to get back together. It took her a few minutes to get herself together before leaving to go pick up Alex.

Lexie couldn't stop the flow of tears as she drove. She parked the car a few blocks from her destination to calm herself before seeing Dani. After walking around the block twice, Lexie could face Dani. *Okay, I can do this. If I just grab Alex and don't mention the divorce papers, I can get out of there without breaking down.*

Alex ran to her bedroom to grab her favorite blanket, leaving Dani and Lexie alone. "Lexie, we need to carve out some time to talk when you guys get back from the beach."

"We don't need to talk, Danielle. I know you want a divorce. I was served with the papers this morning. I will not contest the divorce as long as our custody arrangement doesn't change."

Dani sighed. She didn't want Lexie to find out this way. She wanted to tell her but didn't want to ruin her weekend getaway with Alex.

"Lex, I'm sorry, but you broke more than just my heart when you left, and I don't think I can get past that hurt. I need to get myself back."

Lexie's shoulders dropped in defeat, "I'll drop Alex off at my parent's house Monday morning, and you can pick her up after work."

There were tears in Lexie's eyes when she drove away, and Dani had to turn away to hide her tears. She was meeting Ellie for breakfast, and her eyes were still red when she arrived.

"Hi there, are you okay? What's going on, Dani?" inquired a concerned Ellie.

"My lawyer served Lexie the divorce papers this morning, and it was just hard to see her in pain."

"I'm guessing she isn't the only one in pain."

"It is hard to walk away from my marriage. I do love Lexie, but I know I can never trust her again. The kindest thing I can do is let her go, so she can move on."

The friends enjoyed a breakfast filled with fresh fruit and fully loaded omelets from their favorite diner. During breakfast, Dani told Ellie about her new relationship with Callie, and Ellie was super supportive. She was happy Dani was moving on with her life. Ellie did not miss the days when she would have to literally drag her friend out of bed and force her to shower and eat every day.

"Callie is a sweet girl. I'm happy for you guys."

"She is super sweet. I really like her, and so does Alex."

Walking back to her office, Ellie thought, *oh, Dani girl, what are you doing? You are going to break that poor woman's heart.*

CHAPTER 18

S tanley Darden was still searching for a job. Three months ago, he was a decorated sailor, and now he couldn't even find a job flipping burgers. He missed being in the city of Norfolk. After being discharged from the Navy, Stan moved back home to a small suburb outside of Petersburg, Virginia.

The former sailor had been job hunting all week with no results. It was Friday night, and he needed to blow off some steam. He called some old high school friends, and they planned to meet at a local bar later that night. He even tried to contact his high school girlfriend, but she wanted nothing to do with him.

By the time his friends arrived at the bar, Stan was an entire bottle of tequila ahead of the group. Drunk and frustrated, Stan picked a fight with a bouncer and was kicked out of the bar. One of his friends offered to call him an Uber because he was too drunk to drive.

Stan was escorted to the car by the Uber driver, and in the morning, he woke up with a colossal hangover and no idea where he was. He attempted to stand up and was met with a baseball bat to his ribs.

Gasping for air, Stan sat back down. His head spun, and he waited until he could breathe again before asking, "Who are you? Why are you doing this?"

His captor stood over him wearing an oversized black hoodie and a black ski mask.

"Take the mask off, Chicken Shit, and show me your face!" yelled Stan.

He was hit again, but this time in the back of the head which rendered him unconscious. When he woke up again, his hands were bound together behind his back, and his feet were tied together. His vision was still a little blurry from the hit on the head, but he made out a figure approaching him. He gasped when the figure became clear, and he knew exactly who it was and why he was there.

Lexie and Alex were having a wonderful weekend at the beach. Lexie made every effort to tuck her feelings about the divorce away and focus on Alex. She kept her phone on silent the entire trip. Lexie didn't want to talk to anyone except her daughter for the whole weekend.

After spending a peaceful two days with Alex, it was time for Lexie to face reality once again. She was determined to do two things when she returned to Norfolk. The first was to focus on the good things she had in her life and not the things she had lost. The second was to catch the Mermaid Murderer. Alex fell asleep an hour into their drive back, and Lexie took this time for one last cry.

It's okay. I'm okay. I can do this. I must keep it together for Alex. This is what Dani needs to do to heal from the pain I caused her, and I have to let her do it even if it destroys me.

Broken-hearted but resolute in her decision, Lexie gathered her strength and drove home. It was late when they arrived back in Norfolk. Alex was cranky and wanted out of the car, and Lexie knew she was in for a long night. Alex had slept most of the ride home, but now she was wide awake and wanting to play. It took Lexie another few hours to tire the toddler out before she could finally go to bed.

Lexie was sound asleep the next morning when her phone rang. Startled, the exhausted detective reached for her phone and fell off the bed. *Why is this damn phone always ringing? It's too early to talk to anyone.*

A smile spread across her lips when she noticed the call was from Dani. *Now, Dani is calling me first thing in the morning, which means she must have been thinking about me while she was in bed.*

"Hey Lex, I know it's early, but I need to tell you something. Callie rented an apartment while she was here visiting. She is moving into her new apartment today. I'm going over to help her get settled."

Lexie was at a complete loss for words and was saved by her call waiting. "Hold on a second, Captain Harris is calling."

"Good morning, Detective. You need to get to the station as soon as possible. We have information on Madison Price. Your partner is already here."

Lexie flipped the conversation back to Dani. "What do you mean, Callie is moving here? Why did she rent an apartment in Norfolk when she lives in Wyoming? Just tell me what's going on between you two," raged Lexie.

"I seriously don't have time for your self-righteous indignation. You always seem to forget it was your decisions, and yours alone, that got us here. I never lied to you, Lexie, and I don't appreciate you accusing me of it. Callie reconnected with her family in Richmond when she was visiting, and she wants to get to know them. I think this will be good for her. I have to go now. We can talk later if you want."

She is right. It is my fault we are separated, but she seems to forget we are not divorced yet. Lexie kissed her baby girl goodbye and promised to pick her up when she was done at work. Driving to the station, Lexie passed Callie's new apartment and saw Dani walking up to the front door. Lexie's heart sank. All she wanted was for Dani to be walking up to her front door, not Callie's. That wasn't going to happen today, and she needed to focus on the case.

Jordan met her in the parking garage. "We have to get over to the Navy base. Madison Price has been officially reported missing. Turns out she never went on any mission, and no one has seen or heard from her since she slipped us that note."

Perplexed, Lexie asked, "How did you find all this out?"

"I called in a few favors last night. Senior Chief Rowe is now on administrative leave for lying to the police and withholding information pertinent to a missing persons case. He will not be around to block our investigation anymore," grinned Jordan.

This time, when they arrived at the naval base, they were met by the Master-at-Arms, who was more than willing to assist them in whatever they needed.

"My apologies, Detectives. You understand that I was only following orders?" offered the man.

Jordan asked for the list of names of anyone who may have had contact with the missing girl or either of the murder victims.

After gathering the list, they called and asked the individuals to come down to the station to make a statement.

Once the people came to the station, Lexie noticed she hadn't seen the young woman from the barracks that informed them that Madison was missing.

"Hey Jordan, have you seen the girl from the barracks? The one who showed us Madison's room?"

"No. I haven't seen her. She may be coming in a little later. I really want to get her statement, though."

After five hours of interviews and taking statements, Lexie was mentally beaten. They were no closer to finding their missing girl or the killer. No one seemed to know anything about the two murder victims, but everyone had a theory about Madison's disappearance.

"Several of the statements say an unidentified male was lurking around the building where Madison worked, and she was seen arguing with this same guy yesterday," stated Jordan.

"Let's gather the five people who made those statements and see if there is anything else they can remember about this guy," instructed Lexie.

Two hours of interviewing the sailors revealed that the guy was a white male around twenty-two years old. He had sandy brown hair and was approximately five-foot-seven inches tall with a medium build. One witness said he looked like a weightlifter.

"Maybe this guy is our killer, and Madison knew it, so he took her to keep her quiet," offered Jordan.

Lexie responded, "Or he killed her, too."

Chapter 19

After months of running into dead end after dead end, Lexie mused, "Maybe the killer was arrested on a different charge and is in jail or dead."

Jordan shirked, "Maybe. It's weird that we have two murders and then nothing. Maybe it was personal, and the killer got what they wanted and moved on."

Callie and Dani started dating a few weeks after she moved to Norfolk. They were happy, and Lexie was miserable. She hated everything about Callie, and the tension between her and Dani had never been worse. They couldn't even be in the same room for more than ten minutes without fighting.

The mermaid killings faded from the headlines, and it seemed the city was moving on, but something about it gnawed at Lexie.

Jordan was fixing his third cup of coffee in the break room when Lexie breezed in, "I don't think this is over. It feels unfinished," she announced.

"What feels unfinished? My coffee? I put cream and sugar in it," teased Jordan.

"Not the coffee, asshat. The Mermaid Murders."

Jordan sighed, "I really hope you are wrong, Lexie."

The rest of their shift was filled with catching up on paperwork and reviewing witness statements from the two Mermaid Murders. Lexie was meeting Dani to pick up Alex after work. She was excited to see her little munchkin. She enjoyed her time with their daughter, but she was getting to the point where she wasn't as excited about seeing Dani. *I love Dani with all my heart, but love is painful and disappointing. I'm not sure it's worth the effort anymore.*

The minute she saw her wife, Lexie's resolve vanished. *Dammit, Danielle, why do I still get butterflies when I see you? I want to hate you so I can move on, but I just can't. That smile still melts my heart.* Lexie watched Dani laughing and playing with Alex. They were running through the yard playing tag. Lexie sat on her front porch, waiting for mother and daughter to finish their game. She did not want to take away even a tiny amount of time from Dani because she understood that their time with Alex was even more precious.

Dani finally made her way to the front porch, where Lexie sat. She handed her Alex's bag, "She wanted to bring her new favorite blanket. Also, I need to warn you that she has been asking why she has to live in two different houses and why don't we live together anymore."

"What did you tell her?" inquired Lexie.

Dani smirked, "I told her to ask you. I broke her heart once before when I had to tell her you were gone. I'm not going to be the one to do it again. This is all you, Jolene. You need to tell her something soon. I need you to sign the divorce papers, please."

Before Lexie could respond, Dani was out in the yard kissing Alex goodbye.

It took Lexie an hour to calm down before she called Dani. "We need to have a serious conversation, Danielle."

"I have nothing else to say, Alexandra. We have said everything."

Lexie was in tears now, "Dammit, Dani, we have a lot to talk about. We have not had a meaningful conversation since we left Wyoming. We talk, but you don't listen or try to understand. You cannot just throw me aside without even talking to me about it," cried Lexie.

"Why not, Lex? That's exactly what you did!"

Lexie wanted to scream into the phone, but instead, she simply requested, "Please, Danielle, talk to me."

"Fine. We can talk in the morning, but you may not like what I have to say," agreed Dani. "You can stop by my house after you drop Alex off on your way to work."

"I will see you in the morning," assured Lexie.

Lexie tossed and turned all night in anticipation of her meeting with Dani. She was wide awake when her alarm clock sounded. In her excitement to get to Dani's, she forgot to pack Alex's favorite toy to take to her Grandparent's house. Lexie ran back in and got it. By the time she finally got to Dani's house, she was late for work and frazzled. She called Jordan to let him know where she was if he needed her.

Dani was just getting out of the shower when Lexie finally arrived. She opened the door in her towel with wet hair.

I miss taking showers with you, thought Lexie as she walked in the house.

"Sorry, you were late, and I assumed something came up, or you changed your mind about coming over."

"I forgot Alex's monkey and didn't realize it until I was dropping her off at Mom's house. I had to go all the way back home to get it and take it back before coming here. I would never change my mind about something this important."

"You can have a seat. I'll change and be right back."

Lexie noticed pictures of her and Alex all over the place, but only one of them as a family. It was a picture of her, Dani, and Alex dancing at their wedding. She noticed a picture of Dani and Callie sitting on the end table. Dani noticed Lexie staring at the photo and saw the pain in her ordinarily bright blue eyes.

"Callie gave me that picture a few days ago. I didn't intend for you to see it," explained Dani.

Lexie sighed, "I know you are hurt and feel betrayed. I can't begin to imagine the pain it caused you when you thought I died. I understand there are no words I can say to make the hurt go away. There is nothing I can do to make the betrayal less brutal. All I can do is show you that I'm here for you and Alex, and I'm not going anywhere. I love you, Danielle. I'm not signing the papers."

Dani lowered her head before speaking, "I love you too, Lex, but I can't trust you. I am terrified of what will happen if I let you back in. I know myself, and I know I can't handle losing you again. It's better if we try to remain friends. At least it is for me. I'm sorry, but this is the way it has to be."

Lexie pulled her wife into a strong embrace and held her for a brief time until her cell phone rang, and she realized she was now over an hour late for work.

"I have to go now. Thank you for talking with me and for your honesty," said Lexie as she walked out the door.

Dani stopped her, "There is something else I need to tell you. Callie and I are dating. I'm sorry if that upsets you, but we are getting divorced, and I need to move on."

Lexie had no fight left in her. She simply wiped a small tear from the corner of her stormy blues eyes and walked out. Her silence spoke volumes, and Dani heard her loud and clear. *Damn, has she finally given up?*

CHAPTER 20

The man's wrists were bloody as he pulled against the zip ties holding his hands together behind his back. His ribs ached where his attacker repeatedly kicked him. He knew what was coming, and he knew why he was here, yet the terrified man still begged for his life. His captor was merciless and unfeeling as the knife sliced through the victim's body and blood splattered everywhere.

"By this time tomorrow morning, Stan the man, you will be laid out, naked for the world to see. You know what, Stan? I'm going to leave your tiny pecker on so everyone can see it and have a good laugh."

Three months after the first murder, the Norfolk Police were still searching for the murderer. Madison Price was still missing with no leads on her whereabouts. Lexie and Jordan were the lead detectives on the murder case. They were also working the missing person's case because they assumed Madison was taken by the same person who killed Matthew Stanton.

It was a beautiful, crisp fall morning as 911 dispatcher, Renee Sampson, headed to work. She saw a frantic woman running from the park and nearly hit her when she dashed out in the road. She looked toward the area the woman ran from and saw the body of a black male flopped over the mermaid statue.

Renee called 911, reported the crime, and went to see if the man was alive. He was blood-soaked and completely nude. She wanted to cover the poor man, but she knew she couldn't contaminate the crime scene, so she just stood there waiting for the first responders.

Lexie and Jordan arrived at the crime scene just as the patrol officers pulled up. The officers secured the scene while Lexie talked to Renee. They got her complete statement and sent her on her way. She was not able to identify the woman that ran out in front of her. The woman wore sunglasses, a long black jacket with a hood covering her head and most of her face.

"We are spinning our wheels and running in freaking circles. It's been six months since the first murder, and we have no leads and nothing to go on. Now we have a third victim, and Madison Price could end up on one of those mermaids soon," whined Jordan.

"Or Madison Price could be the one killing these guys," responded Lexie.

"Do you really believe that tiny woman could wrangle these big boys and have the strength to heave them up on the statues?"

"I don't know, Jordan. Maybe Madison and the weight-lifting guy are working together. If we could find either one of them, we could ask. Maybe we should stop whining about what we don't have and go find something that will help us," fussed Lexie.

The detectives drove back to the station in silence. They were chasing an elusive serial killer who had already murdered three men. Both detectives were frustrated, and it put a strain on their relationship.

It was Friday, and both detectives were off for the weekend unless the Mermaid Murderer showed up again. Dani was also off for the weekend, and Lexie hoped to spend some time with her and Alex.

She called Dani, "Hi there, how are you? I have the weekend off, and I was wondering if you would like to join Alex and me at the zoo tomorrow?"

"Callie is starting her new job tomorrow, so I'm free. I would love to. I think it will be fun. Thanks for the invite."

Lexie bit back the words she wanted to say and instead smiled and said, "Fantastic. We will pick you up in the morning."

The trio spent a wonderful day at the zoo, and by the end of the evening, Dani remembered the reasons she fell in love with Lexie. They laughed and talked the way they did when they first fell in love.

Lexie felt it too, "Would you like to stay for a drink after Alex goes to bed?"

Dani grinned, "I would love a drink."

The two women tucked their little angel in and told her three bedtime stories before she finally went to sleep. Lexie poured the younger woman a glass of wine, and they sat on the sofa. They fell into a conversation easily. Lexie talked about the case she was working on, and Dani told her all about a massive fire they put out a week ago. They talked until two in the morning.

"You look really tired, Lex. Maybe I should go and let you get some sleep."

Barely able to keep her eyes open, Lexie agreed. "Today was great. Thank you for hanging out with us. I needed this."

Dani stood to leave and leaned down to kiss Lexie on the head, "Thank you for inviting me. I needed this, too. Alex is growing up so fast. I feel like between splitting time between our houses and work, I'm missing everything. I'll see you soon. Good night."

Chapter 21

Monday morning, the detectives were back with clear minds and fresh eyes. Captain Harris gathered everyone in the bullpen. "Our third victim has been identified as Stanley Darden; a nineteen-year-old white male who just happened to be recently discharged from the U.S. Navy."

"Imagine that," huffed Lexie. "Another dead former sailor."

"What happened on that last deployment? Whatever it was, it must have been bad. That's why no one will talk about it or even acknowledge it," Jordan mused.

"It doesn't make sense for a young man to join the Navy in 2020 and be discharged in 2021. Correct me if I'm wrong, but when a person joins the military, they join for more than a year at a time," offered Lexie.

"Let's see if we can get access to the victim's personnel records," instructed Captain Harris.

The detectives were not able to retrieve the victims' personnel records without a warrant. Since Darden was from Petersburg, VA, Lexie, and Jordan took a little field trip. Arriving at Darden's former high school, they were greeted by the assistant principal and guidance counselor.

"Welcome, Detectives. My name is Anita Albright, and I'm the assistant principal here. This is our guidance counselor, Mr. Webb. Stanley was one of our best and brightest. We are happy to help in any way we can."

The detectives introduced themselves and asked, "Do you know anyone that would want to hurt Mr. Darden?"

Mr. Webb spoke up, "Stan was a prince at this school and in his community. He was always helpful, especially with the younger kids. He made sure they stayed out of trouble. I don't see why anyone would want to hurt him."

Lexie jumped in, "Did he always want to join the Navy?"

Ms. Albright answered, "Yes. His grandfather was in the Navy for twenty years, and Stan worshiped him. Wanted to be just like his granddad. He enlisted when he was seventeen but couldn't go to basic training until he turned eighteen. It's all he ever wanted to do."

With a quizzical look, Jordan continued questioning, "If that was his dream, then why was he discharged from the Navy after only serving one year?"

"Something must have happened there to make him want to leave. I guess figuring that out would be your job," offered Albright.

"Thank you both for taking the time to speak with us. You have been very helpful."

The detectives drove the ninety minutes back to Norfolk, contemplating different theories as to why this upstanding young man found his way onto the mermaid statue.

After arriving back at the station, Lexie and Jordan pored over all the statements they took from the sailors after Madison went missing. Still, there was no mention of any of the victims.

"There has to be someone that will talk to us about that deployment. We need to get back to the base," said Lexie.

"Someone knows something. We will find them even if we have to question every single person on the base," declared a frustrated Jordan.

The Detectives pulled their sedan into the parking lot and informed the Master-at-Arms that they were on base. Jordan attempted to explain what they were looking for, but the uniformed man dodged the detective's eyes and picked at his fingers.

"I'm sorry, Detective, but there is no one here for you to talk with. I'm going to have to ask you to come back at another time."

"What are you talking about? There are thousands of people for me to talk to here, and I plan to speak to every person until I get the information I need," spat Jordan.

"Before you speak to anyone on the base, you will need to have a warrant. You need to leave now, Detective."

Jordan was livid when he got back to the car and explained what happened to Lexie.

"Well, it's obvious they are hiding something, so lets get that warrant quickly and get back here," Lexie replied.

It took two days to get the warrant. "Who knew there was so much red tape to talk to military service members?" griped Jordan.

The detectives, along with several patrol officers, headed for the naval base. They were anticipating a battle, but the warrant allowed them access to most of the base.

Chapter 22

The firehouse was quiet, and Dani took advantage of the downtime to get some sleep. She and Callie were getting closer. Dani enjoyed being with her new girlfriend, but still, she missed Lexie. No matter how much she missed Lexie, she couldn't see a future with her anymore because the trust was gone in their relationship.

Dani was fifteen hours into her forty-eight-hour shift. Callie was taking care of Alex until Lexie got off work. Callie picked up dinner and took Alex to see her mom at the fire station. Dani was happy to see Alex and Callie, but her thoughts always went back to Lexie these days, and she couldn't stop them. Dani felt guilty when she was with Callie and thought about Lexie.

After Callie and Alex left, Dani took a nap. A few hours later, the alarm sounded. The firefighters were on their trucks and out the door within minutes. Truck Sixteen was first on the scene of the fire. Dani and the newest rookie, Max, were the first off the truck. Max was eager to prove himself as more than just the new kid, so he was often reckless. Piper was his training officer, but she wasn't working this shift, so the responsibility fell on Dani.

Max headed full speed toward the burning structure as Dani yelled for him to slow down. There was so much noise that Dani didn't hear the first gunshot. Max hit the ground, and Dani heard the second shot as she threw herself over the injured rookie.

"What the fuck is happening?" whined Max.

"Some lunatic is shooting at us. Are you hit?"

Before Max could answer, the police swarmed the area in search of the shooter. Max was rushed away in the ambulance, and Dani was pushed back behind the fire truck. Once the police secured the scene, the firefighters worked quickly to put out the fire in what ended up being an abandoned building.

Lexie was still on the naval base when her cell rang, "Hey Lex, there was a shooting at a fire call. I wanted to call so you wouldn't be worried when you heard about it. I need to go now. Be safe," said Dani.

"Thanks for calling. I'm happy to hear you are okay. Please be careful out there. This city is full of crazy people, and you have a special talent for finding them," joked Lexie.

Lexie and her partner found a sailor with information on the missing Madison Price. "I'll tell you everything I know, but not here," said Petty Officer Frost.

Lexie guided the Petty Officer to their vehicle, and Jordan drove them back to the station.

In the interview room, Amanda Frost told them what had happened on their last deployment. "One night while we were in port, Lizzie Monroe and I were exploring the city when Lizzie got a text from Matthew Stanton inviting us to a bar. She didn't want to go, but I insisted it would be fun. We went to the bar, and I had a few too many drinks. Lizzie didn't like to drink alcohol, and she wanted to leave, so Stanton and two other guys offered to walk us back to the ship."

Lexie perked up, "Let me guess, the other two guys were Robert Baker and Stanley Darden?"

Amanda continued, "That is correct, Detective. While walking back, we went through a dark alley where Stanton pinned me against a wall and tried to kiss me. I was so drunk that I threw up on him. He was angry and hit me so hard he knocked me out. When I came to, I saw Darden on top of Lizzie. She was screaming and fighting, but Stanton and Baker held her down. I tried to help her, but Stanton pushed me face-first into the ground and held me there. I couldn't see anything, but I heard another man's voice."

"Did you recognize the voice?" questioned Jordan.

"Yes. The man asked if everyone had their turn with little Miss Perfect yet, and I knew right away that it was Senior Chief Rowe. After he was sure the three guys had taken a turn with Lizzie, then he took his turn."

With tears streaming down her face, Amanda continued, "He killed her with his bare hands. They gang-raped her, and then Rowe strangled her. Stanton held my face and forced me to watch Rowe kill Lizzie. The senior chief never looked at me, and I never saw his face, but I know it was him. After he left, Stanton, Baker, and Darden beat me to within an inch of my life. Before leaving me in a puddle of my own blood, Stanton told me to be very careful of how

I handled myself from that point on. Darden let me know if I told anyone about that night, I would end up just like Lizzie."

"Does anyone else know what happened that night?" questioned Lexie.

"I'm ashamed to say I never told anyone. I was terrified they would do the same thing to me."

"This is not on you, Amanda. You are the victim here. Do you have any idea who would want these men dead?" asked Lexie.

The traumatized woman spoke softly, "The thing is, everyone seems to love those guys. Until that night, I always thought they were a great group of sailors; always nice, polite, willing to help whenever needed."

Captain Harris opened the door, "Detectives, can I speak to you both in my office?"

Harris informed the Detectives, "Your witness needs to stay here until I can make arrangements for a safe house. You two need to bring in Rowe for questioning and find out if this has happened to anyone else on that ship. We also need to find out where they dumped Lizzie's body."

CHAPTER 23

The sun was barely above the trees when they arrived at the naval base. The Master-at-Arms greeted the Detectives at the front gate, "How can I help you this time, Detectives?"

"You can tell us where we can find Senior Chief Rowe. We need to speak with him immediately, and we need all the information you have on the disappearance of Lizzie Monroe," answered Lexie.

"Chief Rowe hasn't shown up yet. He is usually here by 0600, but I have not seen him this morning. As for Ms. Monroe, she did not disappear. As far as we know, she deserted the Navy, her fellow sailors, and her country," spat the officer.

Lexie's eyes widened, and her cheeks flushed bright red as she attempted to control her temper. Noticing this conversation's impact on his partner, Jordan gently guided Lexie away from the sailor and back to the car.

"Why is everyone here such an asshole? I hate this place!" yelled Lexie loud enough for the Master-at-Arms to hear her displeasure.

"I see the year you spent on the ranch didn't help your hotheadedness," laughed Jordan.

"Shut up, asshole, and drive," responded Lexie with a grin.

Driving back to the office, the detectives were called to a crime scene. Another male victim had been found slung over a blood-soaked mermaid. Jordan turned the car around and headed to the address they were given. They pulled up to Towne Pointe Park near the Elizabeth River.

The crime scene overflowed with patrol officers, the medical examiner's office, and hundreds of potential witnesses. Lexie remarked, "Let me guess, the victim is Senior Chief Rowe."

Jordan ran his hands through his hair and shook his head as he realized Lexie had nailed it. Rowe was the fourth victim of the Mermaid Murderer. His body was draped over the mermaid that was on the front entrance to the U.S.S. *Wisconsin* at Nauticus. *What a great place to display the body of this monster,* mused Jordan as he canvassed the area.

Lexie joined him, but they knew they wouldn't find anything. The last three crime scenes were meticulous. The killer was intelligent and careful.

"You know, I'm not really sure I want to catch this killer," declared Lexie.

Jordan laughed, "If what Amanda said is true, then I agree. Too bad we don't have a choice in the matter. Our job is to catch and arrest the killer, no matter who it is or why they did it."

After hours of talking to people and searching for some kind of clue, Jordan and Lexie went back to the police station to check on their only witness. Amanda had been taken to a local safe house and was protected by two detectives that Lexie trusted to keep their witness safe.

"I'm going to go check on Amanda before I go pick up Alex. We will get back at it in the morning, partner," reported Lexie.

Lexie rushed home after checking on Amanda. She wanted to get the mac and cheese started for Alex, and she hoped Dani would want to stay for dinner. The doorbell rang, and Lexie beamed as she opened the door, expecting to see Dani. Her shoulders dropped when she found Callie standing there holding Alex's bag.

"Dani asked me to drop Alex off because she was called in early for some kind of meeting before her shift," explained Callie.

What the hell, Dani? You can't take one minute to call and warn me that you are sending your flying monkey to deliver our daughter?

Lexie thanked Callie and quickly hugged her daughter before calling her estranged wife. "Is everything okay, Dani?"

"Yes. All good here. We just had a briefing on the recent shooting and what precautions are being taken to keep the firefighters safe while we do our job. You are upset about Callie bringing Alex to your house, aren't you?"

"Not upset, just a little disappointed. I was hoping to see you," explained Lexie. "Stay safe out there, Dani."

"I'm always safe, Lex, and you need to get used to Callie being around. I like her, and so does Alex. She is a good person. I'm not expecting you to be happy that Callie is here, but I do expect you to be civil when you interact with her. She is helping me with Alex. You should be grateful."

"Grateful? Why should I be grateful that you are allowing another woman to help raise our daughter? She already has two mothers. Don't you think that's enough? I can't have this conversation with you now. I have to go."

CHAPTER 24

The atmosphere in the firehouse was somber after the chief finished his briefing.

"It truly sucks that someone would take advantage of our vulnerability while we are trying to fight a fire and save lives. What the hell is wrong with people?" questioned Piper.

"I wish I knew why people do the shit they do. You wouldn't believe the crap I saw when I was a cop," sighed Dani.

The next few hours were spent cleaning the firehouse. It was quiet until Max started singing, and Dani joined in. Piper started a conga line, and suddenly everyone was laughing and having a great time until the alarm sounded.

The trucks and ambulances were loaded and on the way to a structure fire a few miles away. The Fire Chief reiterated the safety protocols as the firefighters sat in their vehicles anxiously waiting for the police to arrive.

"This is bullshit!" shouted Max. "There could be people in that building, and we are supposed to just sit here while they burn!"

Dani leaned in close to Max, "if you want to fight this fire, you need to calm down and follow protocol, or we will leave your cocky little ass right here in the truck. Understand?"

Max calmed down and waited for orders to exit the truck. The police showed up and secured the perimeter with officers on the rooftops of surrounding buildings. After giving the green light, Dani and the others hit the ground running. They moved quickly to make up for the time they had lost. Dani and Max were inside, attempting to clear the building. At the same time, Piper and the other firefighters worked on putting the flames out. The building was a daycare. Fortunately, it was after hours, and all the children were gone. The only people still inside were the two sisters that owned the daycare.

The younger sister, Alison, was trapped beneath a large pile of rubble. Her older sister, Maryann, was searching frantically for Alison when she heard Dani call out. Max helped Maryann out of the burning building and left her with the paramedics.

By the time Max found Dani, she had already managed to remove the rubble from around Alison. With Max's help, they freed the woman only to find her not breathing. Dani remained calm, and they got her to the paramedics.

Once the building was cleared and the fire was successfully extinguished, the firefighters filed back into their trucks. They were pulling into the station when the first shot was fired. Everyone took cover the best they could inside the truck as the driver tried to get the fire truck into the bay.

A few feet from the bay door, the truck stopped. At first, no one knew what happened, then Dani realized Max had been shot. She rushed to the young firefighter who had been driving the truck and pulled him to the back seat while Piper drove the truck into the bay and shut the doors. The bullets continued to fly until the bay doors closed. The paramedics were still at the hospital, dropping off the two women from the fire.

Dani and Piper tried in vain to save Max, but unfortunately, there was nothing anyone could have done. He was shot in the heart and died almost instantly.

Lexie was sleeping soundly when her cell phone rang. She groaned when she saw Jordan's face pop up on the screen.

"What do you want now, Jordan?" groaned Lexie.

"There was a shooting at Station Six with one fatality. We need to get down there now. I know you have Alex. Do you want to meet me there?"

"I'll be there as soon as I drop Alex off at my parents' house. Do you know anything about the fatality? Is Dani okay?"

"I'm sorry, Lex. All I know is Dani is the one who called 911, but I don't know who the victim is."

Squad cars and lights were surrounding Station Six when Lexie arrived. She saw Jordan when she parked the car, but her only focus now was finding Dani. Lexie tore through the station and finally found Dani standing in a corner talking to someone on her cell phone.

Dani ended her call when she saw Lexie, "Hey, Lex. Are you working this case?"

Despite everything that was happening, Lexie couldn't stop the spread of the smile covering her face. *I love this woman, and I don't know what I would do if I lost her. I now understand why she is so hurt by the FBI faking my death.*

Dani blushed when she noticed how Lexie was looking at her. *Why do I still get butterflies when she looks at me this way? Damn it, Lexie, you make it so hard to be upset with you.*

Lexie walked closer and held out her arms. Dani hesitated for a moment, then fell into her wife's waiting arms. The two women held the embrace until they were interrupted by Jordan.

"Sorry to interrupt, but we need to get going," announced Jordan.

The women reluctantly pulled apart. Lexie kissed Dani on the forehead before walking away to join her partner.

"So, that was interesting. Are you ladies getting back together?" pried Jordan.

Lexie sighed, "I have no clue what Dani wants or is thinking. I want my wife back more than anything, but I can't get my hopes up. Right now, we need to focus on finding out who is shooting and killing our local firefighters."

Dani was reliving the embrace she just shared with Lexie when her cell phone rang. She felt guilty when she saw it was Callie. Not wanting to talk to Callie, Dani sent her a text: *Can't talk now. I'm not hurt, but there was a fatality. I won't be home tonight. Call you later.*

Dani didn't wait for a reply. She put her phone in her locker and went to find Piper. The fire chief was getting everyone together for a briefing and to speak with the chaplain.

"Has anyone spoken to Max's parents?" asked Dani.

"We are sending officers to their house now," answered the chief.

Dani requested, "Please call them back. I want to tell Max's parents. He was my responsibility, and I should be the one to do it."

Piper chimed in, "You are my responsibility. I'm coming with you."

The two firefighters drove to their destination in complete silence. The only sound came from the GPS. Dani thought she was prepared for what to expect when she informed the parents, but she was wrong. She met Mr. and Mrs. Nevin a few weeks ago when they came to the firehouse to see their son.

Piper rang the doorbell, and Mrs. Nevin opened it almost instantly. She smiled when she saw the firefighters, but her smile faded when she noticed the look on their faces.

"Where is Max?" she asked.

Piper couldn't handle it and excused herself from the conversation. Dani asked the confused woman if she could come inside and speak to her and her husband. Mr. and Mrs. Nevin stood as still as statues as they listened to Dani explain what had happened to their son.

It took all Dani's strength not to break down and cry with them, but she knew she needed to stay strong. It wasn't fair for the grieving parents to have to console her in their time of loss. She stayed as long as she could and then quietly showed herself out.

Piper was a wreck by the time Dani made it back to the car. She began apologizing as soon as Dani opened the car door.

"You have done nothing wrong, Piper. This is a terrible situation. We are all just doing the best we can."

After spending the night canvassing the area around the firehouse and interviewing anyone and everyone willing to talk to them, Lexie and Jordan finally called it a night at four am.

Lexie wanted to see Alex but knew it was better if she went home and got some sleep. However, she was too exhausted to sleep. Lexie spent an hour tossing and turning before she finally fell into a deep sleep. She dreamed of Dani, which turned into a nightmare where Dani was shot and killed.

Dani's shift was ending when she saw Lexie pull into the parking lot. She rushed out to meet her wife. "What are you doing here? Are you working?"

"Well, good morning to you too, Danielle. I'm here because I wanted to see you. I needed to know you were safe."

"Thank you for checking on me. I'm okay. We had a tough night, and it's only going to get worse until we find out who's using Norfolk Fire Fighters for target practice. Do you guys have a suspect yet?"

"Not yet, but we will find the asshole. Hopefully, before anyone else gets hurt," replied Lexie.

"I'm starving. Would you like to join me for breakfast at the café?" inquired Dani.

"Yes. I would love to join you," grinned Lexie.

After being seated at the restaurant and ordering breakfast, the women fell into a comfortable conversation.

Walking to the parking lot, Lexie felt hopeful. She informed Dani, "I don't have to be at work for another few hours. Would you like to come over?"

"I'm not ready for alone time quite yet."

Lexie beamed, "Does that mean that you may eventually be open to the idea?"

BULLETPROOF

"Only time will tell."

Chapter 25

E ven though she was working two homicide cases with no leads on either, Lexie couldn't contain the joy she felt after talking to Dani the night before. She felt like Dani was finally coming around and would forgive her soon.

"What's with that silly grin, partner?" inquired Jordan when he handed Lexie a cup of coffee.

Before Lexie could answer, Captain Harris yelled, "Detective Carr, grab your partner and get your asses in my office now!"

Lexie and Jordan reported as ordered.

"Amanda Frost is missing. She disappeared from the safe house sometime late last night," informed Captain Harris. "We promised this scared young woman we would keep her safe. We need to keep that promise. Do what you have to do to find her."

The Detectives went to the safe house hoping to find something that could help lead them to the missing girl. They talked to the officers who were detailed to protect Amanda. Officer Kendrick and Bullard had the day shift.

The officers told Lexie that Amanda wasn't feeling well the night before and went to bed shortly after dinner. "She was fast asleep when Wilson and I took over at midnight," said Officer Pittman.

Wilson spoke up. "Everything was quiet at the house, but when I went to check on the girl at two am, she was gone. There was no sign of forced entry. All the windows were closed."

After getting all the information they could from the four officers, the detectives were at a loss.

"Do you think she left on her own?" proposed Jordan.

Lexie sighed, "At this point, Jordan, I have no idea what's going on here. She was deathly afraid of all the victims. Maybe now that they are all dead, she isn't afraid anymore."

Back at the police station, Lexie was rereading Amanda's statement when her cell phone rang. She was excited to see it was Dani.

Lexie answered the phone, "Well, hello there, Danielle."

"Hi, Lex. How's your day going?"

"Much better now," beamed Lexie.

"I was calling to see if you wanted to have dinner tonight. Just you and me."

Lexie felt her heart skip a beat before answering, "Yes. Absolutely. When and what time?"

Dani smiled. "My place. My shift ends at six o'clock. How about you come over around seven. I'll get takeout."

"See you at seven. Have a good shift and stay safe."

Dani felt a little happier when she went back into the firehouse until she overheard the captain discussing Max's funeral service. The funeral was in a few days, and she dreaded it. Not wanting to think about it, she asked Piper to run some drills with her. Dani was at the top of the hundred-foot ladder when the alarm sounded.

The firefighters of Station Six welcomed the distraction of the fire call. Everyone was saddened by the loss of their rookie. The call was for a house fire in a newly developing neighborhood. There were several houses under construction, and a fire had broken out in one of them. By the time the fire trucks arrived, the entire house was engulfed in flames. There were two fire stations dispatched to the scene. Several police officers were there to secure it and ensure the safety of the firefighters.

The firefighters were on the ground fighting the fire when Dani saw a figure on top of the burning building. She attempted to inform Piper and the rest of the crew, but the fire raged, and the noise was insane. She ran back to the truck to grab an extra oxygen mask for the victim.

Grabbing the mask, Dani turned and felt a sharp pain in her shoulder. The injured woman tried to get help, but she lost blood too fast, causing her to lose consciousness. Before she realized what was happening, she felt another sting in her stomach, and that's when she realized she had been shot twice.

A few minutes passed before Piper noticed Dani was missing. The fire was finally under control. Piper asked, "Has anyone seen Watkins?"

Office Reynolds yelled, "Watkins is here, and she's hurt."

The paramedics rushed to the firefighter's side. One paramedic worked to stop the bleeding while the other grabbed the stretcher.

"We need to get her to the hospital now. She has already lost way too much blood!" yelled the paramedic.

Piper jumped in the back of the ambulance and called Lexie on the way to the hospital. Lexie didn't answer the call because she was jumping in the car with Jordan, heading to the scene of the fire. Piper called Lexie again once they made it to the hospital.

This time Lexie answered, "Hey, Piper. Where's Dani? Is she hurt?"

"I'm sorry, Lexie, but she was shot twice and lost a lot of blood. Dani is in surgery now. That's all I know," reported Piper. "Can you get here soon?"

"I'm pulling into the parking lot now."

Jordan pulled the car up to the Emergency Room entrance, and Lexie jumped out. "Thanks for the ride, partner. Go find the son of a bitch that shot Dani."

"We will find him, Lexie, I promise. Go check on your girl, and give her a kiss for me."

CHAPTER 26

Callie was rushing through the emergency room door when she ran smack into Lexie. "What are you doing here Lexie? Dani is no longer your concern,"

Lexie ignored the jealous woman's ranting and went looking for Piper. Callie was right on Lexie's heels when she rounded the corner and saw a group of devastated firefighters.

"What is it?" asked Lexie.

Piper stood up, "We haven't heard anything about Dani yet. She is still in surgery."

Callie went and sat with the group of firefighters while Lexie paced in the hallway.

Piper followed Lexie into the hallway. "Are you okay?"

"Why is Callie here? How did she even find out Dani was hurt?" demanded a furious Lexie.

Piper sighed, "Callie is Dani's emergency contact. She changed it to Ellie after your death, and when she started dating Callie, she added her and removed Ellie. I'm really sorry, Lex. I thought you knew."

"I knew Callie moved here to be with Dani, but I didn't think Dani was that serious about the relationship. Guess I was wrong."

Before Piper could respond, the surgeon came to the waiting room. "Dani lost a lot of blood, and she had massive internal bleeding from the gunshot wound to the abdomen. We removed the bullet and stopped the bleeding."

Lexie started to speak when Callie jumped in and asked the doctor, "When can I see her?"

"I'm sorry, ma'am, but she will be in intensive care for a while, and only family will be allowed to see her. As soon as she is moved to a regular room, you guys can all visit then. Dani needs to rest so she can regain her strength."

"I'm her wife. Can you take me to her, please?" asked Lexie.

"Of course, Detective. Follow me, and I'll take you to her."

Callie stormed out of the waiting room while Lexie went to see Dani. She was furious that she couldn't see Dani. *This is utter bullshit. Dani doesn't want to see her. She loves me, and I need to make Lexie understand that.* Callie called the person she knew was always there for her.

"Hey Tommy, how are things at the ranch?"

Tommy was breathing hard from running, "I'm not at the ranch Callie, and I'm not even in Wyoming."

Callie laughed, "Where are you then?"

"I'm on a mission to win the love of an amazing woman. I just have to get this one roadblock out of my way."

Callie heard some yelling on Tommy's end of the call, and then she heard the click of him disconnecting the call. *What has this idiot gotten himself into now? Has he chased Ellie all the way to Norfolk?* Callie loved Tommy like a little brother, but even she had to admit the man has issues. She knew Ellie was on the way to the hospital, so she waited in the parking lot for her. Ellie arrived with Cheryl and Dani's parents in tow. Rushing to the entrance, they all stopped when they saw Callie sitting on a bench outside the ER.

"Callie, how's Dani?" asked Mr. Watkins.

Callie looked up at the anxious man, "Dani is going to be okay. I just needed some air. She is out of surgery and in an ICU room."

The group continued their mad dash to the door when Callie asked Ellie if she could talk to her quickly.

"Sure. What's up?"

"Have you talked to Tommy recently?"

"Tommy? Why would I talk to him? We haven't spoken since I left the ranch. He told me that he was in love with another woman at the ranch, and he was spending time with me, hoping to make her jealous. I told him it was cool. I wasn't looking for anything more than a good time."

"Did he say who the other woman was?" inquired Callie.

"He didn't say, and I didn't ask. Look, I really need to go, okay?"

Suddenly, Callie had a sinking feeling in the pit of her stomach. *No, this can't be happening. I need to find Lexie.*

Jordan was called back to the precinct because there was a lead to the whereabouts of their missing witness, Amanda Frost. He hated to leave the search for Dani's shooter, but he knew and trusted the detectives working that case. Jordan called Lexie to fill her in on the case.

"Hey, partner. We caught a break in the case. Amanda has been spotted in the warehouse district. I'm not sure how credible the lead is, but I just wanted you to know that I'm headed there now. How's Dani?"

Lexie responded, "Pick me up at the hospital. Dani will be knocked out for the foreseeable future. There is nothing I can do here but wait and try to control my urge to smack Callie."

"I'll be there in fifteen minutes."

Lexie spoke only to Dani's mother about her leaving. "I need to step out for a short time. We have a lead on a missing girl. Will you call me if Dani wakes up before I get back?"

The older woman continued to hold out hope that her daughter would one day forgive Lexie. She knew, given the opportunity, they would be able to work things out. She disagreed with Lexie faking her own death, but she understood it.

Mrs. Watkins hugged her daughter-in-law, "You will be the first call I make when Dani wakes up. Now go get that missing girl, but please stay safe, Lexie. I worry about you."

Jordan pulled up to the door, "I promise I will be as safe as I can. Take care of our girl until I get back."

Callie was searching the hospital for Lexie when she saw her running out the door. Callie called out, but the detective ignored her and kept going. As soon as Lexie buckled the seat belt in the car, her phone rang. She looked at the caller ID and recognized the numbers as Callie's. *I don't have time to deal with this bitch right now.*

Lexie looked at her partner, "So catch me up, Jordan."

"A man called the tip hotline. He stated he saw a woman matching Amanda's description walking in the warehouse district. The man said he tried to follow her to get a better look, but the woman ran when she noticed him. The caller said the woman ran into one of the old, abandoned warehouses, and he wasn't about to follow her in there."

Jordan and Lexie drove to the area where the abandoned warehouses were and parked the car. Not knowing what was waiting in there, the detectives decided it was wiser to stay together. They entered the building where the woman was last seen. The detectives expertly and carefully cleared each room until they were at the end of the building. Both detectives were frustrated because they felt like Amanda was slipping away, and then they heard it. A small voice from behind the wall.

"Detective Williams, its Amanda. We are coming out. Don't shoot."

Lexie whispered to her partner, "Who else is here?"

Amanda emerged with two other young women. The detectives recognized one of the women as Madison Price, the girl they met during their investigation at the Navy base.

Amanda pulled the third girl out of the darkness, "This is Lizzie Monroe, and together the three of us killed the four bastards who brutally raped, beat, and left her for dead."

CHAPTER 27

C allie tried to call Tommy a few more times, but there was no answer. She called Lexie again, but this time her call was sent straight to voicemail. Frustrated and scared for her friend, Callie didn't know what to do next. She knew she needed to tell someone about Tommy before he killed Dani, but she couldn't bear the thought of something terrible happening to her friend.

Dani was still sleeping when Callie made her way back to the injured woman's hospital room. Her heart sank when she walked into the room. Seeing the once vibrant, strong woman lying there so frail and lifeless was too much for her. Callie turned to leave and ran into Piper.

"Hey, slow down before you end up in a hospital bed, too," joked Piper.

"Piper, I need you to call Lexie for me. I need to tell her something important, but the bitch will not answer her phone when I call."

Piper snickered, "Well, do you blame her? You are trying to steal her wife."

"I'm not trying to steal anyone. I fell in love with the woman that she tossed away. Now she wants her back, and I'm the problem, right? We don't have time to debate this Piper, I need to talk to Lexie now."

"Lexie is going through a lot right now, and I'm not going to help you make it worse."

"Then help me save Dani. I know who the shooter is, and I need to get the information to Lexie so she can stop him from trying to kill Dani again!" screamed Callie.

Piper pulled her cell phone out and dialed Lexie's number. Lexie answered on the first ring.

"Hey, Piper. How's Dani? Is she okay?" asked Lexie in a rushed voice.

Taking the phone from Piper, Callie spoke up, "Dani is fine for now, but we need to talk."

"Callie, this is really not a good time. I'm working and don't have time for your crap."

"Listen, Lex, I know you are busy, and Callie is not your favorite person, but I think you should hear her out this time. For Dani's sake."

Lexie stepped outside the warehouse, "What's so freaking important, Callie?"

"I know who shot Dani and killed Max."

"What are you talking about? Who is the shooter, and how do you know about it?" demanded a confused Lexie.

"Before I tell you, I need your assurance that you will not hurt him, and you will be the one to arrest him."

Lexie was angry, "I will not promise you a damn thing. Now tell me who the fuck shot Dani."

"Why do you always have to be such a bitch? I just want to make sure you don't hurt him. I know the shooter and he is not a monster or a murderer. He lost his way and I'm sure he never meant to hurt Max."

"Fine. I promise. Now tell me the shooter's name, please."

Callie closed her eyes and fought back the tears, "Tommy. The shooter is Tommy. He is in love with you. He believes if Dani is out of the way, then you will love him back. He is in pain and needs help."

All the blood drained from Lexie's face as she realized what was happening. *Tommy. No! This cannot be happening. I need to find him.*

"Lexie? Are you still there?"

"I'm here. Are you sure it's Tommy? Where is he now? This is insane, Callie. Why would he want to kill Dani? He knows I do not love him. This makes no sense?"

"Please don't act all innocent here, Lexie. You need to make this right. Find Tommy and get him to turn himself in before anyone else gets hurt," pleaded Callie.

CHAPTER 28

Lexie was still in shock when she walked back towards the warehouse entrance. She needed to find Jordan and fill him in on the Tommy situation. Lexie almost forgot about the young women until she discovered her partner lying on the warehouse floor with his hands zip-tied to a pole.

"What in the hell happened here, Jordan?"

A groggy Jordan responded, "I'm fine, Lexie. Thanks for asking. What do you think happened? Can you please untie me?" whined Jordan. "Shit Lex, what took you so long out there? I could have used my partner here. Now we have three murderers on the loose once again, and this time they may have disappeared for good."

Lexie explained her conversation with Callie to Jordan before asking, "Is this really such a bad thing? Do we honestly want to find them? How can we blame those three women for doing what they did? Those men did unspeakable things to Lizzie and left her for dead. I say we focus on finding Tommy before he hurts anyone else."

"Agreed," was all Jordan needed to say to let Lexie know he was in complete agreement with not mentioning what happened at the warehouse.

Lexie pulled out her cell and dialed Ellie's number. The phone rang four times, then a familiar voice answered, but it wasn't Ellie.

"Abby? Why are you answering Ellie's phone? Where is she?" questioned a confused Lexie.

"We just pulled her car out of a ditch, and her cell was on the seat. I saw your face on the caller ID, so I answered. There is no sign of Ellie anywhere. Her purse and cell were still in the car with the keys in the ignition. It's like she just vanished into thin air," informed Officer Abby Knight. "We received a 911 call about a car that had run into the ditch. The caller informed us there was a woman in the car that may need medical attention, but when we arrived on the scene, there was no one in the vehicle."

"Where is the witness now?" inquired Lexie.

"There was nothing and no one here when we arrived except this abandoned vehicle in the ditch."

Jordan and Lexie went to the hospital to check on Dani. Lexie also wanted to talk to Callie. She hoped the woman might help her figure out where Tommy was hiding and if he had anything to do with Ellie's disappearance. Dani was awake and talking to Callie when Lexie walked into the room. Neither woman looked very excited to see Lexie.

"Callie, can I speak to you outside, please?" asked Lexie.

"No, you can't. If you have something to say to Callie, you can say it in here," responded Dani.

Before Lexie could respond, her cell phone rang. She didn't recognize the number but answered anyway.

"Well, hello there, beautiful. I have missed hearing your sweet, sexy voice," breathed the familiar voice.

"Tommy. Where are you?" inquired Lexie.

Tommy chuckled, "I will tell you where I am as soon as you tell your precious Dani about us."

Lexie attempted to leave the hospital room when Tommy yelled into the phone, "Don't you dare try to run away from this. Put me on speakerphone so Dani can hear our entire conversation. Every time you lie during this conversation, Ellie will pay for it with a small piece of flesh for each lie."

"Tommy, please, you don't have to do this. I will tell her everything, but you need to let Ellie go."

"Speaker. Now," demanded Tommy.

Once Tommy was satisfied that Dani could hear the conversation, he began. "Tell her about the first time we made love, and don't leave out a single detail."

Fire shot from Dani's usually soft brown eyes, "You slept with him?"

They heard Tommy laughing on the other end of the phone. "Oh, Danielle dear, we most certainly did not do much sleeping that first night. Did we, Babe?"

Seeing the hurt and anger in Dani's eyes, Lexie hesitated until she heard Ellie scream out in pain.

"Tommy, please let Ellie go. I can take her place. I'm the one you want."

"I want to hear you tell Dani that you love me and not her. Tell her how you needed me and how I was the one that saved you, not her. Tell her the truth, and I will allow you to take Ellie's place here with me."

Lexie looked at Dani and Callie before speaking slowly, "A few months after I got to the ranch, I was having a bad time and missed you terribly. Tommy noticed I was upset, so he brought me dinner. He was so sweet and understanding. After almost a bottle of wine, I kissed him, and one thing led to another until we ended up in bed together. We had sex all night that night and regularly after that for another few months. I needed him, and he was there. I finally told him we had to stop."

With a mixture of disdain and fury, Dani yelled, "Get out, Lexie. I don't want to see you ever again. If he hurts Ellie, I will make sure you pay for it for the rest of your life."

Lexie walked out of the hospital and asked Tommy for his location. "I promise I will come alone. I have nothing left to lose. You have taken everything from me, Tommy."

Tommy smiled, "You don't need anything else, my love, because you have me. I will see you soon. I can't wait."

Lexie drove to the motel where Tommy was holding Ellie. She felt lost but determined to at least save Dani's best friend. Lexie pulled the car into the nearly empty parking lot and turned the lights and engine off. She called Tommy to let him know she was there.

"I'm so happy that you finally came to your senses, my love. We are in room seven."

Lexie took a deep breath and knocked twice before Ellie opened the door. Ellie was terrified and had a minor laceration on her face but appeared okay otherwise. Tommy stood closely behind Ellie with a knife pressed against the woman's lower back. Lexie noticed the knife and eased her way into the room.

"Okay, I'm here now. You can let her go, so we can be together. I've missed you so much, Tommy."

Tommy was hanging on Lexie's every word when Ellie twisted around, causing him to lose his balance. Lexie jumped between them just as Tommy was about to stab Ellie. Lexie fell to the floor with blood flowing from her abdomen. Realizing he may have killed the woman he loved, Tommy panicked and ran. He was met at the front door by Jordan and immediately arrested.

Ellie administered first aid the best she could and was relieved when Jordan showed up with the paramedics close behind. Lexie was being tended to by the medics, but she insisted that she was fine and did not need to go to the hospital.

"Lexie, please go to the hospital. You have been stabbed and are bleeding pretty badly," begged Ellie.

"The last time I was in that hospital, they stole a freaking year of my life, and it cost me the woman I love. I can never get that time back, and after this Tommy bullshit, Dani will hate me forever. I would rather bleed out on this floor than to live without her."

Jordan was on the way back to the station with Tommy, who was frantic in the back seat of the police cruiser.

"Is she dead? Please tell me she is not dead. I didn't mean to hurt her." whined Tommy.

"Shut the fuck up man. I don't want to hear the sound of your voice for any reason. You do realize that you killed a young firefighter and nearly killed a good friend of mine. Not to mention, you stabbed my partner. So sit there quietly until I can turn your sorry ass over to booking" yelled Jordan.

Once Tommy had calmed down, Jordan called one of the medics to check Lexie's status.

"Oh, she is being a huge pain in my ass and refusing to get in the ambulance. We stopped the bleeding and got her patched up," reported the paramedic.

Jordan was thankful that Lexie was going to be okay. It had been one hell of day and he was exhausted. He checked his rearview mirror and saw Tommy looking at him intently.

"I know I'm going to jail, and its okay because if I can't be with the woman I love, then I don't really have a reason to be free."

Jordan asked, "Why did you feel like you had to get rid of Dani? She and Lexie are not even together anymore. Dani is with Callie."

"It's not about who Dani is with. It's about who Lexie loves and will always love. She spent so many nights crying by the river. I watched her and listened to her talk to a picture of her and Dani on their wedding day. Lexie would always say, "I will love you until the day you die," explained Tommy.

Lexie finally agreed to ride in the ambulance with Ellie. The kidnapped woman needed to be checked out by a doctor, and so did Lexie. She decided to go if they guaranteed she would not be given any medicine that would knock her out. She wanted to be fully aware of everything happening to her.

Lexie and Ellie were taken to an exam room and checked out by the emergency room doctor. Lexie refused to be seen alone, and Ellie agreed to stay with her. After a thorough medical evaluation, some stitches for Lexie, and a few hours of observation in the ER, both ladies were released.

Leaving the emergency room, Lexie asked, "Are you okay, Ellie? I know you have been through hell tonight, and I'm so sorry for what happened."

"I don't blame you, Lexie. Tommy made his own choices. I know you had a rough night too, but I would appreciate some company. I don't want to be alone tonight, and my go-to person is in the hospital."

"My place or yours?" asked Lexie.

CHAPTER 29

Three days after Lexie's run-in with Tommy, she and Jordan were called to the station. They arrived to find Lizzie Monroe, Amanda Frost, and Madison Price in the interview room. Captain Harris met the detectives at the door.

"These three women walked into the station and confessed to committing the Mermaid Murders. They waived their right to an attorney and stated they would only speak to you two." Informed Harris.

Before entering the interview room, the Detectives shared a confused look.

"What the hell? Why would they come back?" asked Jordan.

Lexie sighed, "Because they are decent and good women who did a terrible thing for a good reason."

It only took a few hours for the DA's office to offer a plea deal that the three women happily agreed to take. They were all sentenced to court-mandated therapy for PTSD. The sentence was lenient mainly because the women turned themselves in and the mental state each one was in after the trauma they all endured at the hands of the four men.

After her recovery and release from the hospital, Dani showed up at Lexie's house with their daughter.

"I'm taking a few weeks for myself to process everything that has happened since I discovered you were alive," announced Dani.

"Sweetie, I don't think it's a good idea for you to be traveling by yourself so soon after being released from the hospital."

"Please don't call me that, and I will not be alone. Callie will be with me. I need you to understand this, Lexie. Don't call me unless it's an absolute emergency with Alex, and I expect the divorce papers to be signed by the time I get back."

Lexie was going crazy, wondering where Dani was and if she was okay. She wanted to respect Dani's wishes, but she also wanted to know what was going on with her, so she called Ellie.

"Have you heard from Dani at all?"

"Well, hello to you, Lex, and no, I haven't talked to her since the day she left."

"I'm scared, El. She couldn't even look at me when she dropped Alex off, and now she is off somewhere with Callie. She hates me, and I'm sure that no good bitch is taking every advantage of it."

Ellie sighed, "You might want to prepare yourself for goodbye this time. I have never seen Dani this upset before. She seems happy with Callie, and all you guys do is hurt each other. Maybe it's time to let go and move on. Maybe for Alex's sake, you can find your way back to being friends."

The words stung deeply as Lexie tried to fight back the panic and tears. "I've got to go. I'll call you later."

Ellie felt bad for Dani and Lexie. She was friends with them both and wanted more than anything to have them get back together, but she wasn't sure they would make it this time. She decided to give Dani a call to check in and see how she was doing, but the phone went straight to voicemail.

Dani and Callie's getaway was in the Charlottesville area. Neither woman had ever been there, they looked forward to a place that held no memories for them. When they arrived, they realized they were in wine country. Callie booked a few winery tours for them over the next week.

After booking the first winery tour, Callie went to find Dani, who was in the bedroom unpacking.

Dani grinned when she saw Callie standing in the doorway watching her, "I was just about to take a shower. Care to join me?"

Callie whispered, "I would love to join you."

Dani slowly removed Callie's shirt and then her own. Sinking her teeth into her bottom lip, Callie watched intently as Dani teasingly stepped out of her panties and into the shower.

"You coming in?" Dani's voice dripped with excitement. "Or would you like me to start without you?"

Callie was flustered as she attempted to wiggle her way out of her jeans.

"Don't you dare start without me."

In the shower, Dani threw her arms around Callie, pulling her close. She was desperate to drown out the thoughts of Lexie she had fought all day. Dani kissed Callie hard. Their lips melted into one as Dani's tongue searched out Callie's. Their kisses increased intensely until both women throbbed in anticipation.

Dani got impatient, so she took Callie's hand and placed it between her legs. Callie felt the wetness as she slid her fingers inside. Dani couldn't stop the flashbacks of her and Lexie, and it pissed her off. She didn't want to think about Lexie.

Dani pressed her body against Callie's hand, "Harder baby, harder. I need to feel you deep inside of me, now," breathed Dani.

Callie rose to the challenge and gave her girlfriend what she wanted. She thrust harder and harder until Dani's knees buckled, and she crumbled to the shower floor.

"Don't move, gorgeous. I just need a second to regroup," gasped Dani.

Callie did as she was told, and after a few seconds, Dani was hit with another wave of desire. She pulled herself to her knees and positioned herself between Callie's thighs. Even with the water streaming down on her, Callie felt Dani's breath on her as Dani trailed kisses on the inside of Callie's thighs. She grabbed the standing woman's ass and circled Callie's wetness with her tongue.

Callie placed her hands on the shower wall to keep from falling. She moaned with pleasure as Dani licked and sucked fervently until she felt Callie's entire body quiver.

Callie grabbed Dani's head and guided her up until they were face to face. "Damn, woman, that was intense and sexy as hell, but what's the rush? We have all night."

Dani kissed Callie softly on the lips and then made her way down her neck to her breast. Callie's nipples were hard, and she was begging for more.

"Yes, we do have all night, and I plan on utilizing every single minute," smirked Dani as she pulled Callie out of the shower and led her to the bed.

The two women spent the rest of the night with their bodies tangled up together. It was the most exhilarating night of Callie's life, and by the time the sun rose, they were utterly exhausted.

They visited as many of the wineries as possible. They spent time walking through the charming small towns that surrounded the larger city. They went to the mom-and-pop diners and the small cafes around the city. In the evenings, the ladies found the most extravagant restaurants for dinner. They always saved their dessert for the hotel room.

After two weeks of wine, fine food, and mind-numbing sex, Callie told Dani they needed to talk.

"What's going on? Is there something wrong?"

Callie pulled Dani to her and kissed her, "You have to go back to your wife. You can't keep doing this to yourself or to her. She made choices that hurt you. I get it, but she didn't make them to hurt you. She was trying to save you and Alex the only way she could at the time."

Dani tried to speak up, but Callie stopped her.

"Please, Dani, I need to say this, and I need you to let me. You are never going to look at me the way you look at her. I love you, and I know you care about me deeply, but you don't love me. It's okay. I came into this relationship understanding your situation. I never thought you and I would last this long. I am thankful for the time we have shared. It's time to move on while we are still friends. I don't want things to get ugly or for us to start hating each other. I love you enough to know this isn't what you truly want or need. You need Lexie. Now get your ass packed, and let's go get your woman."

Dani was so overwhelmed with emotions that she could not speak. She pulled Callie close and held her tight.

"Thank you," was all she could get out before Callie rushed her to the bedroom and started packing.

They were quiet for the first few minutes until Callie finally broke the silence. "Please don't feel weird or awkward around me. We will never make it as friends if you don't relax and just be yourself around me. I do love you, but you aren't the moon and stars, woman. I will get over you. I need to focus on myself for a while," laughed Callie.

The two women had a good laugh. It took two hours to finally get packed and check out of the hotel. They loaded Dani's jeep and set a course for Norfolk. It was only a three-hour drive back, but it was late, and they wouldn't get home until after midnight. Dani thought it was better to talk to Lexie in the morning. She didn't want to wake Alex.

CHAPTER 30

D ani was up early, pacing the floor, waiting for the right time to go see Lexie. She knew Lexie would be waking Alex up in a few minutes and taking the toddler to her grandmother's house. Dani wanted to talk to her before her shift started. She was awake all night thinking about what Callie said and allowing herself to remember why she fell in love with Lexie and how much it hurt to be apart from her.

On the way to Lexie's house, Dani got a phone call from Ellie. "How was your trip? Did you find what you were looking for, my friend?" inquired Ellie.

"It was great, and yes, I did find what I was looking for. I'm on the way to Lexie's house now to tell her I want to work on our marriage. I love her, and I want to be with her. I want to put the past in the past and start over."

There was a long pause before Ellie spoke again, "Dani, I'm so sorry, but Lexie is gone. That's why I was calling. Alex is with me. Lexie brought her over last night because she didn't want to be around when you and Callie returned. She was devastated when you left with your girlfriend. She told me she finally realized that you didn't want her anymore. You made that painfully clear when you couldn't even look at her."

"Do you know where she is going? Why didn't anyone call me?"

"Honestly, we didn't think you would care. Turn the car around and go back home. Your daughter wants to see you."

Dani hung up and immediately called Lexie, but the call was sent straight to voicemail. *I can't believe this is happening.* She drove back home and met Alex and Ellie in the driveway. Alex squealed with delight as she ran to her mom. Dani scooped the girl up and squeezed her tightly before sending her into the house so she could talk to Ellie.

"I can't go through this again, Dani. I understand she hurt you terribly, and you hurt her. The only difference is the pain she inflicted was accidental and not something she chose to do. Please don't put me in the middle of this. Go inside and spend some time with Alex. She missed you these past two weeks."

Dani didn't have to be at work until the following day, so she took Alex to the beach for the day. They had a great day, but still, Dani couldn't help but wonder where Lexie was and if she would ever answer her phone. She called her several more times throughout the day and kept getting her voicemail. After the beach, Dani took Alex home, gave her a bath, and fed her dinner. Once Alex was asleep, Dani called Lexie one more time.

"Lex, can you please call me? We need to talk. I'm so sorry for the way I acted after the Tommy incident. Please call."

Lexie pulled the car into the parking lot of the hotel. She was determined to get to Wyoming quickly. She drove twelve hours straight and only stopped to sleep for a few hours. Lexie had called the ranch owner to see if there was still a place for her there. He was thrilled to hear she wanted to come back and told her she could have her old cabin if she wanted it.

After six hours of sleep, Lexie was on the road again. She had fourteen hours left to drive, and she wanted to complete the journey that day. Her cell phone was packed in her luggage because she didn't want to talk to anyone. All she wanted was to put distance between her and the pain she had caused Dani. Even though it broke her heart to leave Alex, she knew that she and Dani would eventually work out a custody arrangement. She would see Alex again.

Dani was worried because she hadn't been able to reach Lexie in three days. She continued to call and get Lexie's voicemail. She visited Lexie's parents to see if they knew where she went. Mrs. Williams mentioned Lexie sometimes missed life at the ranch in Wyoming. Dani wondered if maybe Lexie was going there. If so, she already had a two-day head start on her. *I'll catch a flight, and maybe I can get to the ranch before she does.*

Lexie was five hours from her destination. She woke up with a heavy heart and stretched her legs. Lexie wanted to keep pushing, but she could barely keep her eyes open. The exhausted woman pulled into the rest area to get a few hours of sleep so she could make it safely to the ranch. She fell asleep as soon as she closed her eyes and dreamed of Dani.

The view was spectacular. *I guess this place is as good a place as any to say goodbye.* She sat on a bench looking out at the mountains in the distance and began writing.

My Dearest Danielle,

I'm writing you this letter because I know I would never have the strength to say this in person. This past year has been brutal, and it's high time I own my choices. I chose to lie to you and let you believe I was dead. I pushed you away and into the arms of another woman. I can see how happy you are with her, and I want you to be happy, Dani. I promise I do, so I'm moving away and granting you a divorce. I will not pursue you anymore.

I love Alex and will be in her life. I will contact you to set up custody once the divorce is finalized.

I'm sorry,

Lexie

Lexie signed the divorce papers and slowly put the letter in the envelope. *It's really over now. I'm letting her go.* She put the tear-soaked envelope in the hotel mailbox and got back on the road.

Lexie finally reached the ranch at nine the following morning. She went to the front office and was greeted by the entire gang. They were shocked and saddened to hear about Tommy but grateful that Lexie wasn't hurt. The ranch owner informed her that her former cabin was clean and ready for her to move in, and she could stay as long as she needed.

"This is perfect timing because my activities director quit last week. If you are up to it, the position is yours," offered the owner.

Lexie was tired from the trip. She promised to see everyone at dinner that night but needed to get some real sleep. She drove to the familiar cabin, and her heart hurt at the final loss of her old life but was at peace that she had finally let go.

Chapter 31

Dani rushed to the airport to find that the only flight available was a direct flight to Casper, a five-hour drive to the ranch. She was told she could wait two days and catch a flight directly to Jackson Hole, but she couldn't wait that long. The frustrated woman rented a car and set a course for the ranch.

Lexie fell into the bed and snuggled up under the blanket. She wanted to sleep and wake up a different person. A person who hadn't destroyed her family and lost the love of her life. She closed her eyes, and a few minutes later, her mental and emotional exhaustion took over, and she slept.

An hour later, Lexie woke up drenched in sweat from a nightmare about losing Dani and Alex in a car accident. The dream was so vivid Lexie could still hear the rain pouring on the roads. It took her a few seconds to realize she was awake, and the sound of the pouring rain was real. She reached for her cell phone and turned it on for the first time since she left Virginia.

Fantastic! No freaking cell service. I've got to get to the airport and to Dani. I was a damn fool to think I could just walk away from her.

Lexie dashed through the rain, jumping over the massive mud puddles and into her car. She didn't take the time to pack a bag or anything. Lexie grabbed her wallet with her driver's license and credit cards and pulled slowly and cautiously onto the road. *I will drive slowly and carefully. I just need to get to the airport before this storm shuts it down.*

Dani drove well over the posted speed limit to keep up with the flow of traffic when the sky opened, and rain baptized the highway. Suddenly, there was very little visibility, and the car in front of Dani swerved to miss a fallen tree limb. Not having enough time to react, Dani's rental vehicle plowed into the tree limb, causing her to lose control of the car.

The car careened off the road and flipped over into a ditch that was quickly filling with rainwater. Shaken up and unable to see clearly, it took Dani a minute to realize that if she didn't get out of the car soon, she would drown. Attempting to remain calm, she struggled against her seatbelt until the car filled with water.

An elderly couple driving behind Dani had stopped when her car flipped into the ditch. They wanted to help, but the woman needed a walker to stand, and the man was weak from recent heart surgery. The only thing they could do was call 911 and pray.

Seeing car hazard lights on the side of the road, Lexie stopped to see if they needed help.

The rain was slowing down, and the elderly man was leaning on his car. "There is a woman in that car. She can't get out. We can't get her out. We called 911, but she can't wait for them to arrive. You have to help her." cried the man.

Lexie grabbed the seatbelt cutter that Dani made her put in her car after they adopted Alex. She moved quickly to get to the trapped woman. Once she was at the car door, she noticed the glass was already broken, so she reached directly into the car and cut the seatbelt. The unconscious woman fell into Lexie's arms and was pulled out of the water.

By the time Lexie freed the woman from the car, the rain had begun pouring again, and she couldn't see her hand in front of her face. She was dragging the woman out of the ditch when the paramedics arrived and took over.

They rushed the woman into the back of the ambulance and administered CPR. The fire department and police department came on the heels of the paramedics. They called for another ambulance to take the elderly couple to the hospital to be checked out. Lexie identified herself as a detective with the Norfolk Police Department and told them what she could about the incident.

Lexie was finishing up with the officers when one of the paramedics came to the car. "The victim is alive and conscious but not really coherent. We are taking her to the hospital now if you want to follow. She may or may not be able to talk to you when you get there. We found this in her pocket. Looks like she is a firefighter from Virginia."

Before Lexie could process what she just heard, the paramedic disappeared into the darkness, and the ambulance was gone.

Noticing the concerned look on her face, the officer asked, "Are you okay, Detective?"

"Yes. I'm fine. Are we done here?"

Speeding away, Lexie followed the police cruiser to the hospital. The ambulance carrying Dani had arrived a few minutes before. The patient was being assessed and treated by emergency room staff when the police arrived to speak with her. Lexie was frantically trying to find the woman from the crash when she heard the sweet sound of a familiar voice.

Lexie followed the voice to a room filled with doctors, nurses, and police officers. Attempting to see the patient, she walked into the room but was met by a nurse who quickly escorted her out.

"I need to see the woman in that bed, please," begged Lexie.

"I'm sorry, ma'am, but you cannot be in here."

"Please, you have to let me see her. I think that's my wife in that room."

While being led out of the room by the nurse, Lexie heard her name. She snatched her arm from the nurse and pushed her way through the crowd around the patient's bed. Her heart leaped when she saw Dani sitting up in the bed, smiling ear to ear.

"Hi there, sweetie. I was told that a detective from Norfolk, Virginia pulled me out of the car. Do I have you to thank for the heroic rescue? I thought for sure I was going to drown in a damn ditch," grinned Dani. "This is my wife. Could you all give us a few minutes alone, please?"

Lexie stood in shock as everyone cleared the room.

"What happened, Dani? How did you end up in a ditch full of water, and what are you doing in Wyoming? Where is Alex?" demanded a perplexed Lexie.

Dani patted the bed and gestured for the confused woman to sit down. She took a deep breath before speaking, "I ended up in the ditch because something was in the road, and I hit it. It was raining so hard that I couldn't see the road. I honestly thought I was going to die in that ditch. The worst part was that I would die before telling you how sorry I am for the way I've treated you. I am in Wyoming looking for you, silly."

"I don't understand," whimpered Lexie.

Dani's expression turned serious, "A year ago, you asked me to fight for you and for our marriage, but I couldn't do it. I was stubborn, and I let my pride get in the way. Lexie, I have never stopped loving you. You are my beginning, my middle, and if you will have me, my end."

With tears of joy streaming down her face, Lexie kissed her wife and felt the last two years just melt away. She knew without a doubt, their love was bulletproof.

Acknowledgements

A special "thank you" to my two favorite girls, Olivia and Wendy who sacrifice their time with me so I can write these wonderful stories for you guys to enjoy.

A huge "thank you" to Daphne Taylor who keeps me on track and keeps the books coming. Your support means the world to me.

A simple thank you is not enough for the team at Emerald Books who made it possible for this book to see the light of day and for the amazing cover. Thank you, Jessica and Isaac.

Finally, my sincerest thanks to all the readers who have followed the Unbreakable series. I love you all!

ABOUT THE AUTHOR

Melissa Seal is a U.S. Army Veteran who retired after 25 years of dedicated service. Melissa recently discovered the joys of golfing and is working towards that elusive albatross shot. She blogs on Medium, often writing about her everyday adventures as a mother of a teenage daughter. She enjoys traveling with her family and can usually be found somewhere near the ocean. Find her on Instagram, Facebook, Twitter, Medium, Goodreads, and Amazon.

FOLLOW MELISSA

@melissa.seal.14

@sealmelissa

Also follow Melissa on **goodreads**.

Sign up for our newsletter to learn about becoming a reviewer, special discounts, book giveaways, writing retreats, and more!

emerald-design.co/newsletter

Made in the USA
Las Vegas, NV
20 August 2021

28446826R00115